CHECK MATE

JONATHAN M EDMANS

Table of Content

SYNOPSIS

A Mexican drug lord has planned for the largest ever drug shipment to the UK. Part of the plan is to contact his UK contact. This is done by a written sheet of paper. This sheet is to be hidden in the hollowed-out body of a chess piece, a King. Unfortunately, the piece is lost when two boys have a collision. The Mexican decides to get the piece back. Unfortunately, the British authorities have got wind of the plan. The chase is on.......

Chapter One

"Come on, mum we will be late," Paul Dawson was sitting in the passenger seat of the car, his mother putting crutches away on the back seat and looking at him. "Do you want to use your wheelchair when we get there? I think it would be easier to move around, and you will have your hands free." "Yes, Mum, that would be a good idea." Paul smiled at the thought of playing in his first under-thirteen chess tournament. His club had signed him up, and now he was on the way with his mum, Sarah, to the tournament at the local village hall.

Sarah Dawson, into the driver's seat, started up the engine, and they drove off. "Do you think you do well, Paul?" His mum looked forward with anticipation, for last night, the club chairman of 'Paul's club had rung to make sure everything was all right, and he had also told Sarah Paul had a chance of doing well. "I think I have every chance; Mr. Charles thinks I'm a strong player; he told me so yesterday at the club." Sarah smiled, so something had been said, she thought.

They drove on through the English countryside from their small hamlet of Harlingford to the next village where the tournament was, Drayford. The sun was up but not too warm, for it was spring, a March Day and the leaves were turning dark green as they grew to be born for summer days.

Sarah pulled into the car park of Drayford village hall. She was happy the entrance and hall were wheelchair accessible; many places were not, and Paul had to miss out, not just on chess but on socialising with other children. She did feel happy for Paul. "We are here," she said abstractly, as she thought Paul had not noticed, but he had, and as the car was stopped, he was already preparing to lift his legs out. Sarah went to get the wheelchair, and carrying it into the passenger side, she went to help Paul. Paul, however, insisted he did not need help, so Sarah promised not to intervene, and she only watched as Paul placed one hand on the wheelchair and pushed with the other on the passenger seat, lifted himself across, and sat in the wheelchair.

"Alright, darling." Sarah looked at Paul and knew the answer already; Paul sat in the chair and straightened his legs. He lifted himself from the seat and into his chair; once in the chair, he pulled each out and placed them firmly on the footplates. "Already, "Sarah looked at her son and could see his father in him, the dark blonde hair and blue eyes, the upper body already strong, and that would grow further, completely opposite to the lack of growth in the lower limbs. Sarah remembered further the day Paul was born and the shock, and in John, her husband's case, disappointment. The disappointment soon turned to anger as he blamed his wife for the spina bifida. Sarah and her husband had tried to stay together, but John could not, and when Paul was two, he left.

So, it was just Sarah and Paul now. Even the family friends had largely abandoned them because of Paul; no one wanted to know; all her friends, being able-bodied, did not want to be associated with Paul hoping he would go away. But he did not, and Sarah had carried on and made new friends of all types and most with some form of disability or impairment, as they called it, following the social model of disability. Sarah stopped thinking as Paul brought her back to reality, "Come on, Mum, we got to go; the tournament is starting soon." "I'm on the way, darling." Sarah gathered herself and her thoughts and started towards the entrance to the hall, Paul leading. Paul entered the hall and saw Danny, his "bestie," as he called him. Danny waved a crutch with a plastic open cuff that went round his arm as he held the grip. Danny's mother also waved and followed up with, "Hello, you two." Sarah replied with her own "Hello." The two women made small talk as their sons talked chess.

The chatting was still going in the hall when the referee for the tournament turned up and brought the hall to order: "The tournament will start at 9:30 am, and play will continue until lunch; lunch will be at 12:30 pm, and we then resume at 1:30 pm"." I would like to thank Mrs. Turnball of the Drayford 'Women's Institute and her co-workers for providing lunch." With that, the referee, Mr. Francis Scott, started the tournament. Each game was on a timer, as was normal, and each game lasted forty-five minutes.

Paul played his four games, drawing two, losing one, and winning one. The win was particularly gratifying as the parents of his challenger had told their son, "He is less fortunate than you; he may not be able to play as well." Paul saw him off with the Sicilian Defence Najdorf Variation, playing 1. e4 c5 2. Nf3 d6 3. d4 cxd4 4. Nxd4 Nf6 5. Nc3 a6. This led to the challenger's mother crying, "Don't worry, darling, you were the better player; he was just lucky." She also complained to the referee that Paul should only play "with his own type." The referee, seeing trouble, warned the parents of disruptive behaviour. The parents left with the son. He had played only Paul.

Sarah Dawson had seen the entire thing but left it to her son and the referee, reasoning that if the other woman became a problem, she might have to be arrested. Detective Sergeant Sarah Dawson was not going to make a scene, not like that, especially as the referee had dealt sublimely with the woman.

Lunchtime arrived, and Paul and his mother went to the buffet and helped themselves to the food. That was a good game, Paul, a good game; Sarah praised her son as always when he won. "Well, he was not that good, really, Mum; he couldn't figure out a response." Paul started to eat a second sausage roll. While eating this, Paul had an idea: "Do you think I will be allowed to play with my own set, Mum?" he asked. "I don't see why not," she reacted with her usual smile. "Go and check with the tournament ref." So, Paul did just that; he went to find Mr. Scott, who thought the request strange but allowed it on the condition he could, as referee, check the set.

Paul went to get it; he rolled down the ramp from the hall, and having the car keys, he opened the 'car's boot; that is where the set was packed away. He reached in and picked it up. He put the board down the side of his chair and put the box under his jumper. He started off up the ramp; he was halfway when another boy came running out carrying a set also. The boy ran straight into Paul's chair and gave a scream of pain that reverberated around the car park as bone met metal. The impact knocked 'Paul's set on the floor, as well as the other 'boy's set. Some pieces fell out, including all the kings. "Are you alright?" Paul looked at the boy still lying on the floor, nursing his legs. "Yes," said the boy, "let me help you pick these up. "The boy slowly and gingerly got to his feet, and Paul started picking pieces up from his chair.

At that moment, a man arrived. Paul looked at him; it was the other boy's father, who promptly scolded his son, Simon. I told you never to run; now look what happened. The man looked at his son's legs, the little blooded scabs as the metal had met flesh. The man turned to Paul. "I'm so sorry," Paul was about to answer when his mum turned up. "What happened?" she looked naturally concerned. The man answered, "My son Simon ran into your son and came off worse, but it was not your boy's fault." Sarah said they could help; the man declined the offer in a polite way, and with that, they took Simon to their car, mounted it, and drove off.

"Well, that was exciting." Sarah joked, "I wish I had seen it." It's not that important, really; come on back to the games, Mum. With that, the Dawsons returned to the hall.

CHAPTER TWO

While the last rounds were progressing at the tournament, Simon and his dad had reached home in the hamlet of Halbury. Simon Lomax watched Dad David bring the car to a halt, and he often wondered when he could learn to drive; he waited for his dad to speak as he always did at a 'journey's end. "We are here, Simon; you get out and see if Anna is at home." David Lomax thought for a second, "I will bring the chess set; you find Anna." David watched his son enter the house; he got out of the car and went to the boot, retrieved the chess set, and went indoors.

David Lomax was forty-five years old, balding, with brown and thin hair; he was an accountant, and he led a normal life at first sight, unlike the Dawsons (he thought). He had brown eyes, and the only thing that stood out in his life was that he was an accountant to a drug dealer. He was going to work for him now; the dealer had organised a major cocaine deal and had sent the bank details and a contact address and name to Lomax. The details were in a handwritten note hidden inside a King of Simons set. The set had been handed to him that morning in the carpark at Drayford by a nondescript teenager on a bike. Lomax had queried why not use email; the teenager told him it was thought safer to use pen and paper, reflecting now Lomax understood the need for secrecy, and the information itself was critical.

Lomax was by now in the kitchen, and it was here he met Anna; he gave her a kiss and "How was the day, darling?" Anna answered in her heavily accented English, as the lady was Spanish. "Okay, I saw Mary, and we had coffee with Louise." David knew the ladies, Anna's friends, and he was happy for her. He looked at her; she was typically Spanish, with raven long black hair and brown eyes. She was also ten years younger. Lomax remembered they met at a party and soon were dating. Lomax remembered it was soon after his wife had died. She died in a boating accident with her lover when his yacht was hit by a tanker in the English Channel. Soon after David had suggested Anna move in with them, she had, and the arrangement worked perfectly; everybody was happy, and Simon took to Anna quickly.

Is supper ready yet? He asked, "Yes. "Anna started to put the paella on the table, David remembering it was paella night as Simon requested. Before supper, Lomax took the chess set to his workroom to get the note. Sitting down, he opened the box containing the pieces and took the White King out. The top should have unscrewed, but with no movement, Lomax looked at the piece. He realised with horror that suddenly hit him where a thread should have been and where the crown should come off; it was a single piece, not the king that should have been. Lomax suddenly thought of the accident with the boy in the wheelchair; the pieces were on the floor, and the boy had the king with the note in it.

Lomax sat back in the chair, his worktable in front of him with the wrong king right in front of him. He was thinking; he was not sure what to do. He had been told that there was to be no communication except in an extreme emergency, and that meant the involvement of the authorities. He thought, well, no authorities involved, well, not yet. Lomax's mind was swimming, and he felt he was

drowning as he knew he must get a message out. He thought
further and eventually picked up his phone, checked his
contact list, and dialled the number to Acapulco, Mexico.

The Casa Dorada Acapulco

Antonio Cardenas pulled the ringing phone from his
pocket; he looked at the screen, saw it was Lomax, and
frowned. Lomax understood contact only in an emergency;
whatever this was, thought Antonio Cardenas, it must be
serious.

He pushed the "answer" button; he said, "What is it, Mr.
Lomax?" His voice to Lomax sounded threatening, and for a
moment, he thought about saying that everything was fine,
but he decided to tell the truth; he told the Mexican, "We
have the wrong king; my son collided with a boy in a
wheelchair, and the pieces scattered, and now the other boy
has our king piece by accident.".

Cardenas looked at the screen, thinking. His main
thought was first how to tell the boss and second what
instructions he should give to Lomax. The second point was
done quickly; he told the terrified Englishman "Find it and
get it back, and quickly, I will leave it to you how you do it;
you have one month before the shipment arrives." Cardenas
clicked off; at the other end in the UK, Lomax had his head
in his hands, wishing he had never heard of the Mexicans.

Juan Martinez took the news quietly. He was drinking his
coffee; it was 12 pm and 6 pm in England. He put the cup on
the table and looked at his number two. Martinez was two
years younger than Cardenas but looked far older; where

Cardenas still had jet black hair, his was iron grey, his skin ruffled and looking older than the tight skin that was attached to Cardenas, his looking tired as against the alert eyes of the taller man as compared to the short and overweight boss man.

Martinez looked at the other man. "Have you told Lomax to find it?" "Of course." "Let's hope he does, or there is a billion pounds of money gone up in flames." "What do we do if he does not?" Martinez looked at Cardenas with a look of red-hot anger, "We lose the deal, and Lomax loses his life." Cardenas nodded and left Martinez.

Premier Inn Hotel Terminal 3 London Heathrow 3 days earlier. Three men were in the hotel room, Cardenas, a bodyguard, and Tommy Silver, the British end of Martinez's network. The bodyguard stayed silent while the other two talked. "Give this to this man." Cardenas showed Silver a photo of Lomax and handed over the chess set. "Do not fiddle with it; there is a small explosive charge inside," the Mexican lied. "What is it?" 'Silvers's curiosity got the better of him, but the Mexican just said, "Deliver it." He gave the Englishman a glaring look; the bodyguard shifted his weight, exposing a pistol under his suit. Silver took the hint. He stopped talking. Cardenas ended the meeting by not saying goodbye.

The Casa Dorada Acapulco the Same Day

Martinez took the phone call. He was happy; the contact had been made, and things were moving. The package that Cardenas had handed over was a chess set with the king piece having an unscrewable top; inside was a piece of paper, and

on the paper was the name of a London banker who
Martinez knew had worked for drug gangs. What was more
important was the fact that the banker was a cocaine user and
a heavy user; Martinez had plenty for him. There were also
two other bits of information, a bank account number and a
telephone number. The plan was simple: the largest shipment
of cocaine was being shipped to the UK and dispersed.
Lomax was to cover up the drug money and to hand the
chess set to the banker, who was to use the bank account to
launder the money. At the same time, he was to ring the
number and tell whoever it was on the other end whose job it
was to make sure there was no problem at the docks.

It had been thought all this information could have gone
by social media as encrypted. Martinez, however, distrusted it;
ever since a hacker from another gang hacked his computer,
the result was one million dollars lost and a shootout with
Texas Rangers that killed seventeen of his militia and nearly
caught him. Consequently, everything was done by pen and
paper, Martinez seeing to it personally. He liked it this way,
complete control and knowing where the computer enemy
was, the computer-armed enemy having no idea of where
Martinez was. He drank his coffee, sat back in his chair, and
watched the Pacific tide ebb and flow up and down the
beach.

CHAPTER THREE

Lomax poured himself a large whisky. He and his family had eaten, and Simon had gone to his room to read up about chess openings, having been beaten because, as he thought, in the openings he played badly. Anna was on the phone to Spain. Lomax finished the drink and poured another, put the glass on the coffee table, sat on the sofa, and pondered his drink and his problem. Where to start, how to start, it seemed an insoluble problem.

Lomax thought he must have thought for about an hour. Then it happened; he went to 'Simon's room, knocked on the door, and Simon answered, "Come in, Dad." Lomax went in and made his pitch. "Who was the kid in the wheelchair?" Lomax asked. "His name is Paul Dawson. He lives in Harlingford and plays for the chess club." "I see," Simon's father began to have a thought for a second and said, "When is the next tournament?" "There isn't one, but we are playing a league game on Friday at their club," "Paul's" queried Lomax. "Yes, Dad." Lomax breathed a sigh of relief. He had a chance.

Lomax went downstairs, a plan forming in his head, or rather two plans, A and B. Plan A was that Lomax would go to the league match, and while there, he would swap the king pieces while no one was looking and break into the Dawsons car if the set was there. Plan B was more direct and could be brutal. The Dawsons would suffer a break-in, and the set would be stolen along with other valuables to cover the real reason for the raid; after all, just a stolen chess set would seem weird and may arouse too much suspicion.

Southampton Port Office, Ocean Gate, Atlantic Way

"Well, that is as much as we know." Detective Chief Inspector Daniel Smith sat down after presenting the latest information on the movements of the SS Sea Giant, coming to Southampton on 21st March 2024. "Do we know if she is the ship with the cargo?" Ken Blake from His Majesty's Excise and Customs looked at Smith and expected an answer; he was not disappointed: "She may be; all indications point to this, and our source is exceptionally good." Blake relaxed, accepted the details, and went back to his sugar-filled tea. Just then, the chief 'inspector's sergeant, John Butler, walked in. "Morning, Butler, anything new?" "no sir, all quiet," but knew the question would be asked; it always was the way, "anything else, anyone?" Smith closed his file in anticipation of the end of the meeting; it was ruined by Blake, who suddenly asked, "I remember there was an idea doing the rounds of a contact who was to run the operation this end, launder the money, and make sure the drugs went where they were meant to go." "I know, but we had no information, yet it may be false." "Now, is that l?" Blake nodded an acknowledgment, and the meeting broke up.

The Casa Dorada Acapulco

Martinez had been troubled by Lomax and what had happened; Lomax had been told to get the chess piece back. But Cardenas had told his boss Lomax was in a real mess; he thought Lomax would fail. This worried Martinez, and he had been pondering the problem. Now he knew. He needed a backup plan, and the only one available to recover the note and, if necessary, deal with Lomax was Robert Alexander. Martinez picked up his phone and dialled a number that lived in Sydney, Australia.

When Martinez rang, it was 7 pm in Mexico, 12 pm the next day in Sydney, a seventeen-hour time difference being in place. Alexander was at home, having recently come back from Germany after having killed a Turkish gangster who had refused to pay Martinez for a shipment, claiming it was not the real stuff expected. "Mr. Alexander, can you fly to London, England, as soon as possible?" The question was loaded, as it always was, thought Alexander. Of course, he would fly. He answered, "Yes, Mr. Martinez, of course." Martinez sounded happy. "Good. I want you to stay at one of the London hotels near the airport and await my instructions." "Understood," replied a broad Australian accent. "Good till then." Martinez put the phone down.

"Lunch is ready, Paul." Mrs. Adams, the housekeeper, put the chicken and chips on the table. "Your mom will be home soon." Paul came into the kitchen. "Thanks," he started to work his way through the chicken. Why are you at home today"? Mrs. Adams poured two glasses of water. "Teachers are on strike. We were told to stay at home; no cover for us." "Oh, I see, dear." Mrs. Adams sat at the table and thought how bad the education system had become since her school days.

The door opened, and Sarah Dawson appeared. "Hi Paul, Mrs. Adams, just in time, I see." She put her handbag and jacket on a chair and poured some water. "Good day, Mum. Any murders or anything? Paul smiled as some chips disappeared in his mouth. "No, darling, nothing like that, but I got to work this Friday, the day of the league match. I

thought you could go with Dr. Andrews and his boy Stevie."
Sarah waited for the upset and misery, but this time there was
none. Paul just said, "I understand, Mum; it's a pity, but I
understand." Sarah looked at her son and wondered just how
he had matured so rapidly; she felt both happy and sad.
Happy for the maturity and understanding shown as against
other able-bodied twelve-year-olds, but sad that it did have to
be that way. They had a quiet supper and then settled down
for the night.

Lomax was also in bed, but he was not sleeping. Anna,
laid beside him, was happily asleep. Lomax was thinking and
rethinking his plans; he had no real idea which way to go; the
first plan was switching the kings at the tournament or
burgling the Dawsons house. The first option was the
cleanest but not simple; it could all go wrong. The second
option was dangerous; the house would need to be searched,
and the set may not be found, and some may come home.

He tossed and turned all night; in the morning, the light
cast shadows through the window over Anna, who had not
woken up. Lomax noticed his sheets had been lost, and he
found them at the end of the bed near his feet. He had been
sweating, and his skin felt damp. His problem had not gone
away, and he felt bad. He had considered turning himself into
the police but decided against it, as turning himself in would
require him to answer questions, and this would mean that
Anna and Simon would be alone, and that meant they would
be killed first, as they were the easier target. If he stayed out
of police hands, at least he would be killed and no one else.
That was how he figured it. He got out of bed, dressed, and
went downstairs to make breakfast.

He had just finished laying the table when Anna appeared. "Simons is still in bed. You alright?" she asked. She looked concerned; the sheets flung everywhere had told her that her chap had not slept.

"No, I'm fine; just a little work stress, that's all, my love." Lomax tried to sound convincing, but he looked at Anna, and she had a look on her face, a smile and eyes bright and alert; she knew that Lomax was lying, and he would sooner or later confess. But Lomax thought to himself, not now, not this; it is too dangerous. He reiterated, "It's all okay, I promise; it's just the Rockman account; the company wants to leave us." "Is that it?" Anna smiled widely. "You'll find another customer; you always do." Lomax smiled back; the lie about Rockman, and his very secure contract had worked, so Lomax had a breathing space.

Simon appeared in the kitchen; this gave Lomax his chance to escape. "Good morning, Simon, sleep well? Good cereal is already on the table." The family sat down to eat....

While the Lomax household was breakfasting in Australia, it was eight in the evening, and Robert Alexander was just finishing his preparations. He had booked the hotel and plane, packed, and tidied up; now one last phone call...

Chapter Four

It was 9:30 am in Drayford; the rain had just started to pour, and Tommy Silver was sitting at his desk. He was working on an invoice for one of his customers who brought their car in for a service. Now, the work had been done, and the car was ready. Tommy Silver had always loved cars until the day he had gone on his favourite quiz show as a contestant, won, and ended up having a holiday in Mexico, Acapulco to be exact, and there he had met Juan Martinez, and the rest they say is history.

Tommy Silver was a small man, with small features. He was in his late fifties and had iron-grey hair, of thin build, and with piercing grey eyes. He looked out the window onto the forecourt of his garage, which was doing well with the drug money that was laundered through it. He remembered the day when, in the hotel in Mexico, at breakfast time, when he had met Martinez at the buffet, Martinez had introduced himself and shown an interest in the garage. Silver had found out that Martinez was a self-employed man like himself, running farm machinery from Mexico to the USA; only later, when Martinez had got to know him, did Silver find out about the drugs.

That had been towards the end of the holiday; Martinez had taken him to the cellar of his house and had shown him the drug stock he had. Silver remembered the conversation when Martinez had made the proposition that 'Tommy's garage would be good cover for Martinez in Britain; Tommy had at first refused. Then Martinez had explained what would happen to 'Tommy's wife if he did not comply, making the point further by bringing a teenage girl to that same cellar that same day, raping her orally, anally, and vaginally, and then killing her by drug overdose. Tommy had given in, then had taken the "devil's food," as Martinez put it, by accepting one hundred thousand pounds; it had tied them both together.

It was then he noticed his phone was ringing. He opened the mobile and accepted the call. "Yes, Silver's Garage, Mr. Silver speaking." Tommy liked that form of introduction; it made him feel important. "Mr. Silver Robert Alexander here. I am an associate of Mr. Martinez. I'm going to work for him." Tommy froze; he knew of Martinez's hitman and heard the stories. "Yes, Mr. Alexander, what can I do for you?" Alexander told him what he wanted, a gun, and a photograph of the Dawsons, and a photograph of the house back and front. Silver listened carefully and told his caller that he would see to it all and that all would be ready when he arrived in the UK in four days' time. Alexander thanked Tommy for his help, wished him well, and put the phone down satisfied. Silver put the phone down and wondered who Alexander was really going to kill.

Breakfast had been finished in the Lomax house; Anna had gone to work, Simon to college, and Lomax to his office. Getting there, he spoke to Samantha, his secretary, and spoke to the senior partner about a deal made last week by a junior, which was, according to Bob Pattison, the senior partner, needed some extra tax work the junior had missed. But Lomax still had his chess problem; his mind was still whirring like a spinning top. He knew he was no thief, that he must recover the piece quickly and with a minimum of fuss. So, he decided that he must get the piece the next night, Friday, when the league match was on. He would get it during the coffee break; it was traditional in this fixture, first game at five with an 'hour's play, and then coffee and snacks at six. Simon had explained all this, and Lomax had made a plan. Now just to wait.

National Crime Agency Units Citadel Place, London

Detective Chief Inspector Daniel Smith was thinking deeply; he had a problem. He had come into work that morning and had been looking at the latest reports on what had become Operation Silver," which had been the topic when he had been at the Southampton meeting. The ship, SS Sea Giant, was still coming to Southampton on 21st March 2024. The suspicion that she was the drug ship had grown, as had the idea of a contact who was to launder the money and make sure the drugs went where they were meant to go, as Blake had so put it. Now, that was the problem. Before that morning, there had been just rumours, single pieces of evidence appearing, and, no real contact, just odd bits emerging very irregularly.

But now that had all changed now. Two days before in Birmingham, an envelope had been stuck under a windscreen wiper on a police car; the officers had found it and read the contents and handed the envelope to their duty sergeant, who had handed it on until it had ended up on 'Smith's desk. It had confirmed SS Sea Giant as the ship and two other pieces of information: one was a name of some kind; it was "Halbury," and the second was the phrase "Chess Piece." Smith looked at the report dumbfounded; no one had any idea of who the contact was and where they were. The only reason they had any idea of the shipment was because of an American report that said that the SS Sea Giant was a suspect in drug trafficking. There was just nothing else. He decided to liaise with Ken Blake, the customs and excise man. Smith looked at his watch: 11 am. Blake should be in his office.

It was 5 am in Mexico, still dark, but Cardenas was up and dressed and talking to his father. Cardenas was forty-four years old with black hair, dark andswarthy skin, and was of medium build. He was very much like his father. Both men were talking; the subject was Martinez. "He is going for the big one this time, 100,000,000 dollars' worth of cocaine." Cardenas looked at his father; the older man just looked back and said, "You should get out; Martinez is dangerous." "I can't; I have no opportunity; he will kill me; I need to find my chance." Cardenas sounded distraught. "Take the chance when it comes, son." The father put an arm round his son and gave him a hug. Cardenas looked at him and just smiled; he had not been able to sleep, so he had dressed and rung his father, which had led to the meeting. He had work to do.

Smith had been on the phone to Ken Blake for nearly two hours. They had discussed the new information, Blake unable to help with the mystery contact. In fact, Blake asked more questions than Smith; he wanted to know everything, as the contact may have information on the tax status of any businesses in the UK that belong to known or suspected organised crime. However, Smith had no details so far as the current operation was concerned.

After putting the phone down, Smith gathered the file together and reread the information they had. First there was the ship; that was the easy part. It was coming to Southampton, and she may have drugs aboard; he kept an element of doubt. Then there was the letter. "Chess Piece" and "Halsbury." They were completely mysterious. No clue whatsoever. Nothing. Smith realised they could possibly stop the shipment, but they needed to catch the people behind it. That was his real problem. He looked out the window and drank his tea, still thinking of the suddenness of events. It was twelve in the afternoon in London. In Acapulco it was six in the morning.

Martinez woke up; he stared at the mirror in the ceiling the blonde, from last night's party, slept on. Martinez thought about the sex; it was fun; she was skilful. Martinez continued looking at himself; he thought about the recent events; he guessed it was nearly time for the Australian to get to Britain. Martinez wondered about the instructions he had been given. Perhaps when Robert Alexander landed, he should add more, perhaps not. He turned on his side and cuddled the unknown blonde, catching sight of the cocaine line on the bedside table.

Chapter Five

Three days had passed. Life had continued, and the pieces of the puzzle that were to bring different people from different places slowly fell into place. The first was a Cathay Pacific flight that landed at 6:20 am at Heathrow, London. The contents of the plane were dispatched as ever to find baggage and meet whoever; they were the usual Europeans, Africans, Americans, Asians, and' Eurasians'—the world in one place, in this case, the baggage hall, Terminal Five.

One of this mass of humanity was a six-foot-two-inch Australian, muscular, and with blonde hair and blue eyes, to anyone looking, a typical sportsman and outdoor type, and that was what Robert Alexander was. He was wearing a white T-shirt and jeans and had his backpack as hand luggage; he only had two other pieces to collect. On the way he checked his phone; nothing yet. He walked on and collected his baggage, cleared customs and security, and headed for the taxi rank. He soon found one, and giving the driver the hotel address, settled in the back of the cab and planned his breakfast and his telephone call.

While the killer was on his way, the Dawson household was in full swing. Paul had gone to school with a friend, and Sarah was also heading out. Mrs. Adams was cleaning through, as it was her day for cleaning at the Dawsons. Paul, before he left, had reminded his mum tonight was the league match, and that she reminded her son he was going with Dr. Andrews and Stevie; she would not be there. His mother had reminded the son that her job was not that simple, so it went through the usual discussions between the two, both understanding the possibility it would not be they be together because of 'Sarah's work. So, for the Dawsons, the day progressed.

For Detective Chief Inspector Daniel Smith, the last three days had been agonising. No advance on the information received, no other clues, nothing. He really thought of forgetting the entire thing and following any new leads, but there were none. That was until the day that Alexander arrived, and Paul Dawson was having his league match. It had begun quietly. Smith and his sergeant, Butler, had been going through the latest reports and had been due to have a meeting with some visitors who wanted to see the NCA in action. Before that, Butler went to the canteen to get breakfast for himself and Smith. While in the canteen, he overheard a conversation that he never thought he would. The speaker was Detective Constable Angela Lightman. Butler overheard that she was getting married, and she was setting up home after transferring to the Hampshire police in ""Halbury"." Butler reacted fast; he took the stunned Detective Constable to Smith, and Smith asked her about Halbury and Chess Piece. He was told that Halbury was a hamlet of five houses and nothing else; it was an hour from Southampton. As for Chess Piece, she had no idea; the only thing was that there were two clubs nearby, one in Harlingford and one in Drayford, and both villages were only twenty minutes from Halbury and, like Halbury, only an hour to Southampton. With that, Smith dismissed the very nervous detective from the presence of the tall, austere, brown-haired chief inspector.

After she had gone, Butler asked, "Well, what do you think, sir? Hell of a long shot." "Well, it is, but you know, sergeant, we must follow it until we know more." "Smith went on, we will go to the local bods and ask around". Butler looked at his boss and guessed that meant they would be away a couple of days and would have to tell Paula, his other half; he answered, "Yes, sir.".

Robert Alexander, after breakfast, made his telephone call to Tommy Silver; he found out that Silver had a gun and the photos of the house and the Dawsons. Alexander also asked about his living arrangements; he thought about organising before he left Australia but decided to work on Tommy Silver as he knew all about the local area. Silver had told him that he could stay in the garage, as Silver had a side room; 'he'd be okay there. Alexander agreed. Silver said that he would come to London to get the hit man. Alexander agreed to that as well.

The village hall at Harlingford was a traditional building, just a hall with a kitchen, a stage, and a room, big enough to have dancing or indoor sports. Tonight, it had five tables, each with a clock and two glasses for water. There were no boards laid out that would be done just after all the introductions and welcoming the opposing team. At six that evening, the teams began to assemble with their supporters and the kitchen staff, who were to make coffee and tea and provide snacks after the match. Paul and Stevie were among the first arrivals; Lomax and Simon came next.

Lomax had been planning how to do this; the league match would start at six in the evening, with one hour of play, then a break. That would be at seven and last for thirty minutes. That would be enough time; the teams and supporters, drivers, would be eating and drinking. He could slip away and change the pieces, and he would not be seen for the simple reason that the umpire for the evening had put a blackboard to write the results of the games on, and the board was right in front of 'Paul's table; no one could see the table.

Lomax made himself comfortable on one of the many chairs that were stacked against the wall. He waited and watched; his watch said five fifty, ten to six, ten minutes to wait. Lomax suddenly started to get nervous; the thought of theft, even if it was just one chess piece, made him feel bad. His mind wandered back to his Mexican holiday, where, like Tommy Silver, even though he did not know about Silver, he had the same treatment, except Anna was involved.

That, like 'Silver's encounter, had been towards the end of the holiday; Martinez had taken him to the cellar of his house and had again shown the drug stock he had. Like Silver, he remembered the conversation when Martinez had made the proposition that Lomax as an accountant would be good for Martinez in Britain, washing drug money. Like Tommy Silver, Lomax had at first refused. Then Martinez had, as was his plan, explained what would happen if he did not comply, again bringing a teenage girl and, unlike Silver, bringing Lomax's partner Anna to that same cellar that same day, stripping the girl, strapping her to a table, and raping her orally, anally, and vaginally, and then killing her by drug overdose. Lomax, unlike Silver, tried to resist. Martinez had Anna stripped and strapped to the table. Lomax had seen this and had given in; then he too took the "devil's food. accepting one hundred thousand pounds and promising to wash the drug money.

Lomax jerked back to the present; he watched the tables, a sudden feeling of horror that started with a bad feeling in his stomach and rushed through his body. As he looked at 'Paul's table, he saw the pieces; he felt sick as he realised that they were plastic, not the wooden pieces they should have been. Then he knew the tournament last week had different rules; the league match meant that the home team must provide the pieces and boards. Lomax felt crushed; he just stared at the hall in a daze, not knowing what to do, only seeing visions of himself dead somewhere cold and lonely; he thought about what would happen to Simon and Anna; the image of Anna strapped to that table in Mexico rolled through his mind, pain biting him. He would have to think again.

The rain was thundering down, the countryside blacked out by dark clouds, smothering what had been a blue sky. Amongst these continual walls of water, Tommy Silver was nearing the end of his journey. Having picked up Alexander Roberts, they were now ten minutes from Drayford. The journey had been uneventful and largely silent, the Australian only swapping hellos and "had a good trip." Tommy Silver, as he had driven, had a deepening terror of this Australian and could not wait to get rid of him.

Chapter Six

Lomax had driven home with Simon after the league match. He was deep in thought, not knowing what to do, his mind swirling in thoughts about what he was going to tell Martinez and, more importantly, how he would react. Little did he know that the reaction was only twenty minutes from his house...

Robert Alexander had finished unpacking; Tommy Silver had brought food and left. Alexander, now eating, cast his mind back to the instructions he had received from Martinez. First, he was to get the information on the Dawsons; secondly, he was to make a plan; third, if necessary, he was to tie up any loose ends, which means killing anyone who would be in the way. Alexander had also been told to talk to Lomax; Lomax had not been told a thing. Alexander, with the visit to Lomax in his mind, continued to eat his pizza.

The day dawned bright over Police Headquarters in Winchester, England's former Anglo-Saxon capital before London. It was so bright that the blinds were drawn where the windows faced this blazing early morning furnace. One such window belonged to an office occupied by Detective Superintendent Jas Singh, or Jasleen, who had that morning company in the shape of Detective Chief

Inspector Daniel Smith and detective sergeant John Butler. Offering his guests tea or coffee, Jasleen Singh asked his visitors what they wanted. Smith did not hang around: "The SS Sea Giant is coming to Southampton on 21st March 2024. We believe the ship is carrying drugs." "I see," Singh looked at the visitors with a keen eye; he followed up, "And what can we do? That is a customs area of expertise." "I know." Smith Countered, but we have information that this end of the network lies here in one or more of these places". Smith showed the list of place names: Harlingford, Drayford, and Halbury.

Singh looked again at the guests. "Are you really sure?" "Well, we are acting on information received," Smith parried the blow. Singh then said, "What do you want then?" Smith finished his tea and continued, "We need a source that knows these places well that can merge in and keep their eyes and ears open., not particularly undercover, but that can merge." "Someone local then knowing the places well and the people," Singh started on his second coffee. "Yes, precisely, and besides, we have no time for an undercover operation. Know anyone who can do the job?" "Yes, I do." Singh, while saying this, pressed a button on his intercom and asked someone to fetch Detective Sergeant Sarah Dawson.

Five minutes later, Sarah Dawson appeared. "Good morning, Detective Sergeant. May I introduce Detective Chief Inspector Daniel Smith and Detective Sergeant John Butler? Gentlemen, Detective Sergeant Sarah Dawson." "Nice to meet your sergeant, Dawson." Smith eyed the new arrival; she was tall for a woman, just a couple inches short of himself, and he was six feet 1 inch, and she was undoubtedly fit—very physically fit, for not only being tall, she was heavily set, and it was with muscle. "Do sports, do you?" asked Smith; the question was intentional. "Yes, Judo," came the reply. "Good, okay, then down to business," Smith gave Dawson the place name list. She looked at it, though, for a second, and replied, "Yes, I was born in Harlingford, went to school in Drayford, and my parents are from Halbury." "So, you know the places well." Smith narrowed his eyes, waiting for a negative response, but there was none; instead, he got "Yes, I do very well." Smith looked at Dawson and relaxed, "Alright, I will tell you what we want," turning to Singh, "any more tea or coffee around?"

The briefing lasted only about thirty minutes, and Sarah Dawson knew what she had to do: keep an eye out for anyone or anything that was not part of the local scenery. Dawson thought to herself that it was not too difficult after all; the places were tiny.

"I'm heading for lunch now, Mrs. Snow." It had been three hours since 'Dawson's meeting, and Lomax was taking an early lunch as he had a meeting in the early afternoon. He looked at his watch: five past twelve, plenty of time, he thought. Mrs. Snow replied, "Don't forget your appointment at two." "I'll be back before then," Lomaz assured his secretary, who had been with him since he became a partner of Baker, James, & Watson, accountants of Southampton. Lomax walked out of the office and was on the street and could see his target, the sandwich shop at the end of the street; it was his favourite place, mainly because it was the centre of business gossip, and you could always find out something new. He walked towards the shop, unaware he was being watched and followed.

Lomax reached the shop, went in, and found a table in the centre of the room. He sat down and waited for the waitress, who was talking to a male customer who obviously wanted a date, as he was telling the entire world by the volume he was using to win the woman's heart but failing. He caught the waitress's eye, and as she was walking over, a large man came into the shop and headed for Lomax's table. Lomax saw the invader and the waitress. He was about to say something when the stranger intervened, "Mr. Lomax, my name is Alexander. We have a mutual acquaintance, Mr. Martinez. I work for him; we need to talk." The stranger turned to the waitress, "I'm buying honey whatever Mr. Lomax wants; I take one of those mugs of tea and a bacon sandwich." The waitress was more receptive to the denim-clad and blonde-haired stranger than the skinny, dark-haired twenty-something shouting his head off earlier; as for Lomax, he had lost his appetite on Alexander introducing himself. In fact, Lomax was feeling sick. "What do you want, Mr. Lomax? I'm paying." "Coffee," Lomax replied. He really did not want anything; his stomach was churning, and he really felt ill.

"Mr. Lomax, I was sent here at Mr. Martinez's request. I was asked to recover a piece of property that belongs to him and which you know about." He continued, "Please tell me how far you have got with your inquiries." Lomax stared at him, his mouth dry; he thought for a second and decided to confess all, so he did: how the piece was lost, his instructions, how he had failed at the first attempt. Alexander said nothing; just listened. Lomax finished his story and waited for the response. When it came, it was an anticlimax: "Well, Mr. Lomax, no need to worry anymore; I am to take over." Alexander fished his wallet out of his back pocket, ready to pay; he also produced the photos of the Dawson's house. "Is this the house?" He looked at Lomax, and Lomax nodded violently, wishing this Alexander man would go away. Alexander, however, was not finished. "Do you have pictures of the occupants?" Lomax shook his head in the negative, time-honoured fashion, his fear of this man growing by the second. "That's a problem, Mr. Lomax. Can you get them for me?" Lomax did not answer; he felt crushed. He saw that cold, lonely place come nearer; he eventually said quietly, "No.". The Australian glared for the first time. "No matter; I can do that soon enough." Lomax just stared death he thought, not far away. Alexander then said, "I see you, Mr. Lomax; I will be in touch." With that he left the half-drunk coffee and the half-eaten sandwich and left. Five minutes later, Lomax followed, went back to the office, and had a difficult appointment with his customer, his mind being on the stranger.

Alexander was sitting in his car; he was thinking, thinking hard. He needed to work out the Dawsons routine; from what he had been told, because of the son's disablement, life was very different. Alexander, if he was to break in, was going to have to plan his attack when he would be sure he had complete loneliness. He would need those pictures; he would start this afternoon. He was about to move off when his phone rang. He looked at the screen. It was Cardenas. He answered, "Hello, Mr. Cardenas, what can I do for you?" Alexander listened, Cardenas told him.

CHAPTER SEVEN

The Casa Dorada Acapulco

Antonio Cardenas and Juan Martinez talked about what Alexander had been told. "Do you think he can pull the thing off?" Cardenas looked at his boss, Martinez, drinking a whisky, thought for a second, "Well, the fact is we need the merchandise back, and the faster he can do it with minimal fuss and no attention, I believe he can."

Cardenas poured himself a drink. "What about Lomax?" His question seemed to annoy Martinez, who just stared at his number two, "Lomax is a nobody; we can deal with him when we like." He went on and repeated himself. "Alexander is to get the merchandise back, bring it to where it was meant to go, and get out fast."

Cardenas looked towards the Pacific Ocean, deep in thought... What if Martinez was wrong?

Robert Alexander arrived in Harlingford thirty minutes after the telephone call with Mexico. He parked the car in the centre of the hamlet, got out, and stood looking at the five houses and one small shop. He scanned everything quickly; he noticed the entire thing had been built in a semicircle, the five houses, and finally, the small shop, which was open. Alexander looked at the scene again; the house he wanted was number 1. It had two cars in the driveway, and he could see a woman cleaning inside. He decided not to attempt it today; he had about a week before things would be difficult, but he was not worried. He decided to go into the shop and find out more about the place.

He entered the small shop, which was a general store, and saw a teenage girl behind the counter who gave him a nervous smile. He smiled back, and seeing the teenager was interested in the visitor, he said in his best Australian "Hi, my name is Rick Hawkins. My company sent me from Adelaide to here for a five-year stint. I'm in a hotel in Southampton but want to rent a place in the country, anything here." The teenager started to blush; she liked the hunk, as she was later to tell police in sadder circumstances, but for now she blushed. "No, I don't think so. Everyone owns here, sorry," "No matter," Alexander picked up a chocolate bar and asked for a sandwich, paid, and left, but he was already planning his next move when he saw Mrs. Adams, the housekeeper, come out.

He immediately went into his act: "Hi, my name is Rick Hawkins; my company sent me from Adelaide to here for a five-year stint. I'm in a hotel in Southampton but want to rent a place in the country, anything here." Mrs. Adams looked at the stranger and thought and answered, "No, not here, but you could try in Drayford." Alexander smiled and then went further: "I was looking for something like your place. 'It is not my place.' Mrs. Adams looked at Alexander, and unlike the teenager, started to wonder what the man wanted. Alexander sensing trouble, replied, "Thanks, I go to Drayford." Mrs. Adams acknowledged him, wished him a good day, and went to the second car in the driveway, got in, and left. Alexander sat in his own car and looked around again. He saw there was no way he could easily get in through the front, but he did see a public footpath running alongside the houses, and he guessed it ran behind, and he guessed further there would be a parking spot behind the houses.

He started the car, and turning right at the crossroads in the direction of the path, he soon found a car park. He drove and saw the footpath, and then after parking, he saw through the trees the houses. He also noticed a cycle track that gave him an idea. He rang Tommy Silver and asked for a mountain bike.

National Crime Agency Units Citadel Place, London

Detective Chief Superintendent Alan Cartwright was at his desk, reading the latest information on

"Operation Silver." He had been reading for half an hour and was expecting Detective Chief Inspector Daniel Smith to join him to discuss "Silver." He had a lot of questions and wanted answers as his political boss, the Ministry of Justice, was getting excited about journalists asking difficult questions. He had just started to read when there was a knock at the door. "You wanted to see me, sir.".

Detective Chief Inspector Daniel Smith entered and, at Cartwright suggestion, made himself comfortable. Cartwright started the ball rolling. I read the latest information on "Silver," but I want your own ideas," Smith thought and then started with his as it turned his latest word of mouth report. "Well, we know the SS Sea Giant, coming to Southampton on 21st March 2024, and the ship has the cargo, our source is exceptionally good." "Who was the contact, Cartwright had seen there was no name. "The contact was the Ship's captain, he worked in the days of the South American dictatorships in Chile and Argentina, "Is he reliable?" "Yes", Cartwright read a little more. He looked up and said, "What about this Birmingham thing, an envelope It is confirming SS Sea Giant as the ship, and the other pieces of information, "Halbury" and "Chess Piece."

Cartwright listened and when Smith had finished followed up: "You went down there", "yes sir, a long shot true but it is our only real lead, and I did speak to Detective Superintendent Jasleen Singh, we told him about the SS Sea Giant and the ship, is carrying drugs. I suggested the crime network lays here in Harlingford, Drayford, or Halbury." I also asked for someone to go and have a look around quietly, Detective Superintendent Singh, found us just the officer, Detective Sergeant Sarah Dawson, born in Harlingford, school in Drayford, parents are from Halbury." Cartwright back in his chair. "So, what now"? Cartwright asked, "we keep on track sir" Smith explained.

Tommy Silver arrived at his garage with one mountain bike as requested. Alexander was waiting for him, and watched as the bike was unloaded and brought into the workshop. "What do you want this for" Silver tried to make conversation, "Keep out of things that don't concern you; you done what you need to". Silver looked at the Australian who stared back a deep menacing look as he stared blankly as the Englishman. Silver felt a chill of terror, this was one individual you did not question; Silver handed the bike over and left.

Alexander sat down with a bottle of beer and a hamburger, having already eaten the chocolate and sandwich. He had worked out the plan, he would cycle to Harlingford early, leave his bike in the car park, fix his observation point, take a look at the house, wait until all was clear, walk down the path, and enter the house from behind when the housekeeper had gone, he had three days at most to get in. He had all day he thought he could wait the housekeeper after all left at lunch time. Tomorrow was a workday he would start very early to make sure he would be alone.

The Dawsons too were having evening supper and discussing the day. Paul said the school had been okay and he would finish his homework, his mum said she had organised her leave, and that would be in June; they could go and see Uncle Tim in Devon, and Tim having a farm she knew Paul could help feed the animals. She was about to talk further when the phone rang. Sarah picked it up, saying, "Hello Dawson speaking." "Mrs. Dawson, Mrs. Adams, Can I come tomorrow afternoon? My neighbour has a doctor's appointment, and I need to take her." "Well, Paul will be away all day with school, so it should be alright," Sarah waited for a reply; Mrs Adams was happy "Thank you I'm much obliged to see you tomorrow perhaps." Yes, said Sarah, perhaps.

CHAPTER EIGHT

The next day arrived, and before first light, Alexander had cycled to Harlingford, had parked the bike in the car park, and walked along the path. He found his observation point in the woods and could see the back of the house. He looked at his watch; he had two hours before any movement. He would observe, and then, when he had seen enough, he would make his move. He looked carefully for signs of life and could see nothing. He opened the breakfast he had brought with him and ate and drank coffee a little. He finished and put everything back in his backpack, and looking again, he checked his watch: seven thirty in the morning. He could hear the Dawsons on the move; he could see the kitchen, and sure enough, he saw a woman and a boy in the kitchen. The boy was in a wheelchair, as described. The problem was he had no idea of the routine; he had to think quickly. Would the boy be there all day? Would he go to school? Would a second person, as well as the housekeeper, be there?

Alexander waited; he looked at his watch; it said seven fifty. He then heard a vehicle; through the trees, he could see a bus, and as he watched, the boy and his mother came out, and Alexander watched as a lift was lowered and then raised with the boy on it. He saw the bus go, and then five minutes later the woman left in her car, but where was the housekeeper? Alexander looked at his watch; five past eight, he decided he would wait for an hour. He remembered it was about twelve midday when he had seen the housekeeper, so three or four hours' work, she should have been here by now, but not a sign of her.

He began to think about the possibilities and decided. He would get into the house now and go straight to the boy's room and look for the chess set, as Cardenas had told him, and leave. Alexander began to move towards the house. How to get in? He had not brought his lock picking tools; he had not brought his glass cutter. He would have to rough it, but how? His problem was soon to be solved, but the danger increased.

Mrs. Adams was worried; it had been planned to take Mrs. White, her neighbour, to the doctor for an appointment, but she had been taken ill, and her granddaughter had rung for an ambulance. Mrs. Adams had then found herself able to go to the Dawsons, but she had not been able to ring and say anything about the change to the plan, so she had decided to drive to the Dawsons and leave a note when she had finished, and now she was pulling into the driveway when Alexander had seen her. He had watched her get out of the car, open the front door, and go in.

Alexander allowed five minutes and followed and very gently opened the front door; he was standing in the hallway and could hear the woman in the kitchen; she was cleaning and had the radio on. He looked around; the living room was to the right, the dining room to the left, and he could see that the doors were open. He also saw two other doors closed; one was the downstairs bathroom; it said bathroom on the door. The other, he was not sure. He saw the stair lift, so the boy slept upstairs. The Australian decided to look around and deal with the woman if necessary. He would start with the mysterious room.

He took several quiet steps, all the time listening to the woman and what she was doing. She was still working in the kitchen. Alexander opened the door and looked inside. It was a workroom with a bureau cabinet, a table with a computer, and a printer in the corner, but there was something else: there was a shelf, and on that shelf, there were two chess sets. Alexander picked the first box up and opened it. He picked up the white king and tried the head of the figure; it did not move, he put it back and went for the second box. He opened it, took the king out, and turned the head. Nothing, nothing happened. The Australian wondered what to do; it was then someone said, "Who are you and what do you want?"

As Alexander swung round, he was confronted by Mrs. Adams, and he noticed she had a knife. "Don't be a fool, woman." He tried to sound aggressive but was really uncertain; he could not be sure how she had heard him. Mrs. Adams watched and said, "Stay there; I can use this. I heard it when I went to the living room." Alexander then remembered he heard a footstep but thought it was further away; he had been too busy with the chess set. He looked at the woman and made his decision.

He lunged at the cleaner, and being so fast, he knocked the knife out of her hand, and she fell backward. Alexander used both hands on her throat and squeezed; the woman struggled but soon went limp as the air of life went out of her. Alexander let the body drop from the landing to the ground floor. He looked at the dead cleaner now lying on the floor. He listened out for anything or anyone, but nothing. He knew he had to hide the body and put the dead woman where she would not be easily found.

He decided to wrap the body, but how? He went downstairs and had a look for anything that would work. He found nothing; he decided then to go upstairs and find the boy's room. He went up, and at the top on the landing, he saw what he wanted straight ahead; he entered the room, and immediately he saw the chess set on a table, went to it, and picked it up, opened the box, and found the white king.

He turned his head, and nothing happened; nothing. He tightened his grip, but nothing; it did not open. He tried a final time, but it was the wrong piece. He put the king back and went downstairs. He saw the body; he knew he must leave it; that meant he had to get out of the UK fast. He thought a while, looking at the body. He examined the dead woman with professional interest. It had been a good kill; she had died very quickly. He made his plan: go back to his base, contact Martinez with the news, and then contact Silver and organise his escape. The body would have to stay where it was. He looked at the clock in the room; it said 10:30 am. So quite some time before the body would be discovered, he left, went to the car park, and rode home.

He got home and changed, made tea, and pulled a ready meal from the small freezer Silver had set up. He warmed the meal up, the tea had brewed, and he began to eat. He was hungry, and the Indian chicken korma felt good. He drank his tea; the heat of the tea and the spicy food felt good. He was just finishing when he saw Silver; he looked, and he saw a look of concern on 'Silver's face.

Silver opened the door and entered. "We've been looking for you everywhere; I have a message for you here." Silver handed over a piece of paper. Alexander looked; it just said, "Ring me." No name, but he knew who it was. "I'll talk later. Now you got to help me escape. I got what I came for, but I had to kill the cleaning lady." Silver listened in astonishment and began to sweat when he spoke: "It will be difficult, may take time. I'll find you a place to hide in the meantime; you can't stay here." The Australian nodded his agreement. "I will answer the message first, then I will pack, and you take me to the new place." "Okay." Silver, who helped himself to tea, picked himself up from the chair and left. Alexander dialled a number.

Chapter Nine

The Casa Dorada Acapulco

Martinez clicked the phone off. He had heard what the hitman had to say and had in reply told Alexander he was on his own, he had to make sure the document was delivered, and that Lomax had to be killed. Cardenas looked at his boss and asked, "Will he be okay" "Alexander will be alright; he has survived and as long as the police don't get a lead over the cleaning woman, there should be no problem." Martinez put his coffee cup down. "But what if...." Cardenas was asking the question when he was brutally cut off. "I said Alexander will be alright he has to sort himself out we cannot help him; besides he has his further orders, I know he will carry them out". With that Martinez walked out on to the balcony overlooking the Pacific.

In the UK, Alexander was lying on the bunkbed Silver had given him. It had been two hours since his phone call, and his mind was in turmoil, first the dead woman he was sure no one had seen him, but he still had a doubt; he may have missed something, but what, if anything, he was not sure. The second was the Lomax problem. Lomax had been sentenced to death by Martinez and Alexander was expected to carry it out, but bearing in mind the first accidental killing a second one in the same area was just being too risky. The third thing was getting out of the country, alexander knew if he was caught, then he too would have a death sentence. He, however wanted a long retirement with Silvers's help, he could get out of the country. He took a drink from his beer can and started planning Lomax's killing.

When Alexander started planning it was three o'clock, and Paul was being brought home by his taxi, the driver had buzzed the doorbell expecting the cleaner to open it, but instead found the door off the latch and open. The driver when inside and screamed, she ran out and, in her shock, attracted the neighbour who came out to see what was happening. Soon, the police and ambulance were there; they cordoned of the house and waited for the detectives, who soon arrived, the senior being Detective Superintendent Jas Singh.

On arrival, he spoke to the constable, "What have we got?". "A woman, sir, dead and pushed from the first floor over the landing to the ground floor, looks like that". Singh looked at the constable and thought for a second; he remembered this was Sarah Dawsons place; he got the same constable to contact headquarters and bring the detective sergeant here. Sarah Dawson had the news in the canteen at headquarters, she had been having coffee after a particularly difficult interview with a rape suspect who denied everything even though the entire thing was on his phone not deleted. she thought it must have been Paul and she had driven home in fear as to what she would find. But Paul was alive and well, Mrs Adams was, however not.

"Know anything about what could have happened" Jas Singh was intrigued when he learned the victim was his detective sergeant's housekeeper, having been told by the neighbour who had called the police. "Now I don't." Sarah was stunned, stunned at the victim being her housekeeper and stunned the murder scene was their home. "Do you think

there is anything missing" Singhs' question went over
Dawson like waves on a beach, until she said quietly, "I have
to check." She immediately thought of her jewellery, went
upstairs, and checked the jewellery box that had belonged to
her mother. Everything was there. She went downstairs to the
living room looked around. Everything was in place,
television, stereo, computer, DVD player, nothing was amiss.

She went back to her chief a said nothing was stolen.
Singh was lost for ideas, he told Sarah that to kill someone
and just leave was odd, did the housekeeper have enemies?
Sarah said no absolutely no. Jas Singh was not impressed,
surely there must be a reason he ordered a complete search of
the house. The search was soon over, nothing had been
touched and nothing had been touched apart from the third
chess set Paul had taken to school that day....

Alexander finished planning for Lomax's killing. It had
to be fast and at the first opportunity, he decided to track
Lomax each day until he got his chance, it would be in the
same area, and it was a big risk, a very big risk, but there was
no alternative. As for getting out of the country, Silver had
found him a flat and Alexander had told Silver where a
second passport and other identity papers were, Alexander
had the idea when he landed in Britain to hide a second set of
documents in Silvers car in the boot taped to the inside of it,
of course in the short time between then and now Silver had
not opened the boot. As for the new place, he could be there
in one hour. He still thought about the dead woman. He had
thought further and not had seen him. The only question is
how fast the police would be. He knew he had to work faster.

The day ended with the sun slowly going down and the
final rays of sunlight and shadows vanishing by bouncing off

the blinds that belonged to the office occupied by Detective Superintendent Jas Singh. He had been back in his office for about an hour. He had just drunk his third tea, he was thinking over and over and getting nowhere with an apparently motiveless murder. He thought of Sarah Dawson again was it someone with a grudge and the grudge had cost the housekeeper her life? Sarah Dawson was adamant there was absolutely no reason to have killed Mrs Adams, none at all, Sarah herself with Paul were spending several days with Pauls Uncle Tim in Devon, as for her assignment that would have to be put on ice, and he knew he needed to ring Detective Chief Inspector Daniel Smith. It was then the thunderbolt struck him. He remembered the conversation; the London detective had explained the situation and asked for a source that" knows these places well that can merge in and keep their eyes and ears open", Singh remembered what he did next, he summoned Sarah Dawson, the perfect policeman for the requested job, and now her housekeeper was dead. The Detective Superintendent picked up his phone and rang a London number.

Daniel Smith was sitting down at dinner with his girlfriend of two years, a Lawyer when his phone rang; he looked at the number and flipped the green phone on his screen. He was annoyed as this was the first evening he had with Sue; she had been in Scotland, and now for the first time in a week they were together. Smith was not going to move unless he really had to. Sue looked at him, and looked pensive as Smith began to speak. "Smith here", "Hi its Jas Singh from Hampshire; listen I think I may have a lead." He began to explain the whole thing, the possible connection with Smiths' request, the circumstances of the murder, and the fact it was Detective Sergeants Dawsons home. Smith listened, making notes on a napkin; he began to think about what was being said, he listened further then he too had a lightning bolt moment. He realized that it had been only three days between his visit and the murder. Could it be that there was a leak in the investigation? "Listen, Jas I think we may have a problem." "What's that?" came the reply. "Well, Jas, it has been only three days between my visit and this housekeeper's death. Could be we have a leak, a corrupt police officer?". "I doubt it" "Besides, only you, I, your sergeant, and my sergeant are the ones who only ones who knew your request. Singh was firm in his assertion. "I understand." Smith was sympathetic; he continued: "I have privately checked my sergeants record you should check Dawsons. Singh thought for a moment, "OK," his words were delivered with a sound of disbelief, but anything was possible. He said good night and put the phone down.

Chapter Ten

Jas Singh put the phone down. He was still thinking about the possibility that Dawson could be a bad apple. He did not believe it, especially if she was corrupt, having a murder committed in her own house with the possibility of finding something that Dawson would not want found. Dawson was an organised individual, and having a body around was not 'Dawson's way of doing things. No, the killer would have taken the body away on 'Dawson's instructions. He decided to go through it just to check her file.

The meals had been eaten, two boxes of fried chicken, and both men were now on their second beers; Alexander was sitting on one side of the kitchen table, Tommy Silver on the other. "I've been planning what to do about Lomax and getting out of the country," Alexander took a swig from the bottle; Silver looked on and said, "Okay, let's hear it, and what about the dead woman?" "I am sure no one saw me. I thought about it over and over," Alexander took another swig, "I also thought about Lomax. It's risky, but it needs to be done quickly. I'm going to make the hit at his home." Silver looked at the Australian put his bottle down and leaned as though he wanted to listen closely. "You sure this could work? Two murders so close together? Even our police are not so stupid; they make a connection somewhere." "Well, maybe, but it needs to be done fast, and I need to get out fast." Alexander drank the last of his beer and grabbed a third bottle. Silver stared, wondering if the Australian was alright. The hitman saw him and just glared and said, "I will track Lomax each day until I get a chance at his home; timing is important, no drive-by shooting. Did you get the documents in the envelope hidden in the boot of your car?" Silver handed the envelope over and followed with the question, "You like this flat, best I could do in the time?" They had been in the new flat, a small flat with a tiny kitchen and bathroom; the living room was part of the kitchen. "It's all right for my needs." Alexander had been drinking faster; he then asked, "How do I get out of the country?" "By private yacht, you will be taken to Cornwall, and a yacht will pick you up in a bay, and you will be taken to Spain, and then you're on your own; full details after Lomax is dealt with, security you see, my contact does not want anything to go wrong.".

Jas Singh had gone through 'Dawson's file; just as he thought he found nothing, nothing to link her with any South American or Mexican drug dealers, nothing to link her with anything at all, in fact. He wasn't surprised she had been on his CID for two years and had been a good detective. He thought that the killing of the cleaner was either a burglary gone wrong or there was someone else with a concern for operation "Silver." His problem now was who. He decided he needed to speak to Smith in London.

Alexander's meeting with Silver and Jas Singh's checking of his detective 'sergeant's file had taken place the same evening, and the following day, five days after the murder, Alexander was watching Lomax's office and watching his every move because today was going to be the first and probably only chance to kill Lomax. He waited. It was nine-thirty in the morning. He would follow Lomax wherever he went. He sat back in his driver's seat and wondered when Lomax would come out for lunch.

That same day, at the same time, the sun that was shining over Lomax and Alexander shone over Harlingford, and seventeen-year-old Sarah Burton was preparing to work in the small shop her parents had run for the last ten years. She was thinking about all the police activity for the last five days and the discussions and gossip in the small hamlet about the apparent motiveless killing.

Sarah put on her overall with the shop name on it and picked up her smartphone. She looked out the window and saw the sun rising above the trees that were just in front of the car park. Sarah looked at the scene, grabbed her phone, and took a picture; she liked taking pictures of the morning and evening. She looked at the photo app and admired the new picture; she then saw the other, the same kind of morning view, very beautiful but different. She looked at the date; it was the same day as the killing. It was then she noticed the figure. She had taken the photo but had not had time to look; now she was looking carefully and noticed a man at the door of the house where the murder had taken place. She looked closer and recognised the man she had spoken to in the shop, the foreigner.

She rushed downstairs and entered the shop. "What's the matter, love?" Anna 'Burton's mum was just opening the post office desk. "I have the murderer on my phone, the killer of the cleaning lady." Mr. Burton arrived. "You hear that, Dan?" said his wife. "Our Sarah caught a murderer," "cried the teenager. ook." She showed the photo; her parents looked, and the humour that was present was in a second replaced by concern for what was on their daughter's phone. Dan Burton broke the silence, "I think we need to tell the police." He dialled a number and reported the presence of an unknown man at the murder scene early in the morning.

Jas Singh had spoken to Smith. Earlier that morning, before both of them were in their offices, he had presented his theories about the burglary gone wrong or there was someone else who was in on the case. Smith dismissed the burglary for the simple reason that a burglar burgled; this one had not. The other was more like it, for the simple reason that the way the cleaner was murdered was quick and with professionalism not usually associated with a village in Southern England. For his part, Smith had no news and told Singh he had the best chance now of turning something up. Singh agreed and promised to follow up the professional killer theory, but how...

He did not have to wait long; soon after talking to Smith, his phone rang again. He answered, "Yes, Detective Superintendent Singh speaking." "Detective Constable Bell, sir, we have a phone call from the owner of the shop opposite the scene of the crime house in Harlingford. It seems his daughter took a picture that morning of the view from her window and captured a suspect in the picture." Singh listened and then said, "Okay, get me a car, and we'll go now and talk to the photographer.".

Singh was excited as he went to the carpool. What a breakthrough! A face that needed a name—now he was getting somewhere. He met DC Bell in the garage; they drew a car and drove out to the Burtons.

While Singh was getting into his car, Alexander was getting out of his and following Lomax, who had come out of his office early, and instead of heading for lunch, he had walked towards the town centre; Alexander followed. He wondered what was going on. Lomax had been walking and then had gone into what looked like another office. Another accountant, Alexander, followed and watched Lomax enter a ground floor room; he waited a minute, and seeing he was alone, he quickly again followed.

The office had a single desk and was full of filing cabinets and a computer, printer, and phones. There was a second door, and Alexander moved towards it and put his ear to it. He heard a couple kissing and whispering sweet nothings. He put his eye to the keyhole and looked through. He Saw Lomax pulling at the 'woman's skirt and she pulling at his trousers. Alexander pulled the gun with its silencer, his chosen method to kill Lomax, and pushed at the door. It opened, and he fired two shots. The first hit the woman in the chest, and she fell back on the floor; the second shot hit Lomax in the head, and he fell on top of the now-dead woman.

CHAPTER ELEVEN

Alexander looked at the bodies for what seemed like minutes, but it was not; it was only seconds. He recovered his composure, turned round, and left the room and then headed straight out of the building and walked quickly back to his car. He was soon there, and there was no sign of anybody discovering the body, he thought to himself as he climbed in the driving seat. It was then the adrenaline that had overtaken him before now suddenly drained. Alexander put his hands on the steering wheel and put his head on them; he had been such a fool, he thought to himself; he had no doubt been caught by CCTV, and no doubt any witness may have noticed the tall, muscular Australian; he was not very missable. But then he thought further: the woman had been wearing a wedding ring, he thought, and Lomax was obviously a lover, so the entire thing could be blamed in the first place on a jealous husband or a lover; that would give Alexander time to disappear, and that had to be taken care of. He felt sick; he remembered the chess pieces and why he was in the United Kingdom in the first place. He would have to go back this afternoon or tonight and probably have to hold them hostage. He was considering the options when his phone rang...

"Well, thank you for your cooperation and the printout of the photo, very helpful, Miss Burton." Jas Singh was finishing his cup of tea. He had a good afternoon; it was a beautiful photo of a man over six feet tall, very tanned and muscular. No, there were not many of those in the area, but more importantly, the man had an accent—not British

English, but Australian, as Sarah Burton told the detective, as she watched Australian soap operas and could tell the difference between the two accents. Singh thanked her, and he and DC Bell made an exit.

"Well, we have a face and a country, and now we need a name." Singh smiled and looked happy, a breakthrough at long last. "Shall I put the word out, sir?" Bell stared straight ahead, the constant stream of traffic fixing his attention. "Yes, and I also want to find other witnesses; some saw him after he left, 'I'm sure of it." "You want a road check?" Bell asked. "Yes, on the road that goes past the house; someone saw him; someone must have.".

Alexander was looking at the phone; he let it ring, and eventually picking it up, he composed himself in case he had to tell bad news about the chess set, but he did not have to. It was Tommy Silver. "I got your escape route sorted," Silver chirped happily, an obvious weight removed from his mind. He went on, "You will be going by private yacht, leaving Cornwall at the end of the week, as planned, then you go to Spain. "What's with Lomax? "I have killed him, not the way I wanted, but opportunistically. I need to get out later night." The n news shook Silver to the re. "I can't arrange that quickly; we have things to do, people to see, and we have to make sure you get to Cornwall." Alexander listened, then he felt more adrenaline and yelled down the phone. "I've killed Lomax and his girlfriend, two bodies, and I still have to find that document. I need to go back to Harlingford tonight; I have been caught by CCTV and witnesses who may remember me."

Silver was silent at the other end. He listened as the Australian was breathing deeply. He finally said, "Okay, go and get the document, then come to my house. I will hide you in the loft". You can stay there until you need to." The Australian agreed, and Silver told him he would wait at nine that evening for him; the call ended, and Silver decided he had to tell Martinez but was beaten to it.

The Casa Dorada Acapulco

Juan Martinez was angry, very angry, and the target was his hitman. He had sent a message and then phoned Alexander just as Alexander had finished with Silver. Now, after speaking to his hitman, Martinez was thinking of Cardenas's words: "Do you think he can pull this off?"

"Well," Martinez thought, "Alexander had not done so. Three dead people, two of whom shouldn't have died. But, as Alexander said, they could have been witnesses. True, but still bad." The document was still not in Alexander's hands. Cardenas had been right, and Martinez found himself wondering what to do about the Australian.

When Cardenas came into the room, he looked at his boss, Martinez, who was drinking wine. Before he could speak, Martinez interrupted him.

"You were right," Martinez said. "He failed."

Cardenas looked at him and asked, "Well, what are you going to do?"

"What can I do? I trusted Alexander," Martinez replied.

Cardenas picked up the wine, looked at the label, and saw it was red. "You want one?" he asked.

Martinez nodded. Cardenas poured himself a glass of wine and looked toward his boss, who was sitting in his chair with a wine glass on the table, arms resting on the armrests. He seemed to be staring into space, deep in thought, lost in the most profound depths the human mind could reach.

Cardenas remembered his original thought: Martinez was wrong.

It was five in the afternoon, and in the offices of Greenwood and Associates, Katie Lewis was starting work as a cleaner, a temporary job before she went to art college in September. Today being a Wednesday, she was to start on the ground floor as Mr. Greenwood held his weekly team meeting on the first until six. She decided to start in Amanda 'Cartwright's, the secretary's room. She knew that the office would be empty, so gathering her cleaning things, she headed to the secretary's office.

She got to the office and pulled her key out to unlock the door. But as she put the key in the lock, the door swung open, and Katie was left wondering why, normally it was locked, but not today. Could Amanda Cartwright have forgotten? It was an odd thing. It was then she noticed the door to the anteroom where the filing cabinets were. That was ajar, and slowly Katie Lewis went towards it; she stepped towards it and let out a cry of horror, so loud it brought Mr. Greenwood and the rest into the room. "What is it, Katie? "Greenwood was looking at the pale-faced young woman, who pointed to the scene in the room. Amanda Cartwright was on the floor with her skirt pulled up and her underwear pulled down, and on top of her was a man with his trousers and underwear down round his ankles. "Call the police; say there has been a double murder." Greenwood gave the instructions, making a mental note that the woman, his secretary, had been shot in the chest and the unknown man in the head.

The police arrived in the shape of Detective Inspector Peter Allen and Sergeant Fiona Macpherson.

Both looked at the scene and saw that the two were in the sex act when shot. Allen gave his instructions.

"I want to find out where everyone was and about the dead man; we need a name and check for CCTV," he knew there were cameras in the street and in the building. Allen then saw a new woman standing at the door; it was Dr. Andy Davis, the crime scene investigator and medical doctor. "One shot through the head, the other the chest—clean shots." The Dr. was looking at the victims, "They were copulating, and I would suggest the woman was shot first." "Interesting, Andrea," Allen used the doctor's proper name, "When can I have your full report?" "Later tonight I will get it written up and sent.". "Good" Allen turned to his sergeant, who, having gone to check on witnesses and CCTV, had returned. "I have the CCTV disc here with the last five hours' worth, and everyone here has been accounted for. Allen knew this point, as while talking to the doctor, Macpherson had been interviewing the five people that were already present. The undertaker arrived. "Alright, take them away, and let's get back to the station." Allen knew there was nothing more to do here.

CHAPTER TWELVE

"Well, what do you think we have got?" Fiona Macpherson asked D.I. Allen. "Looks like an angry husband who found his wife with her lover, or an angry wife for that matter." Allen Looked at the preliminary report from the doctor; he read aloud, "Two shots, victims hit once each, close range, and the nine-millimetre bullet recovered." Allen thought for a moment and then said, "Do we have the CCTV?" "On the way up, there's a lot of it from the street and the office." Macpherson started reading the report herself. "Well, we will wait on the footage." Allen looked out the window, his mind wondering about the angry spouse who had shot his wife or husband.

Detective Chief Inspector Daniel Smith was fed up; since talking to Singh, the trail had gone cold at his end. Nothing Absolutely nothing had come his way; it could be said "Operation Silver" was dead. Detective Chief Superintendent Alan Cartwright Was also on his back for information, there was not only a week away from Southampton, the Birmingham thing, the envelope concerning the pieces of information "Halbury" and "Chess Piece" had not produced anything else. Even Jas Singh, with his possible connection, was seemingly dead. Even the corruption theory had died. The only thing that stood up was Singh's professional killer theory, and that had only a single leg to stand on. Smith looked at his watch; nearly lunchtime, he wondered whether to go into the canteen or out to a cafe. He was thinking it through when the phone rang. It was

Singh, and he was in a very excitable mood, a very excitable mood.

Earlier that day, Jas Singh had been following D.I. Allen and the double murder that had been reported. He had found Allen watching CCTV, and he had also been watching when DC Bell appeared. "Can I have a word, sir?" Singh acknowledged him and started to move when he saw on the screen the man he was looking for. He turned to the other two detectives. "That's our man! We merge the enquiries: Allen, you lead as boots on the ground, and Bell, you work with him". I think we got a good chance at last of getting somewhere". Singh was about to leave when he saw the phone on the desk; he suddenly decided to ring Smith in London.

Smith was listening to Singh and his mood; Singh explained about the new murders, and the suspect was the same as in the killing of the cleaner. He also insisted that there must be a connection between these murders and "Operation Silver." Smith agreed and asked for a picture of the suspect. He also told Singh that once he had it, he would send it out and see who knew or may know the suspect; he did not know how long he had before the suspect vanished from Britain, as it turned out events were to move fast, very fast, indeed....

Alexander looked at his watch; it read eight. It was evening, and he was preparing to break into the Harlingford house. He had seen a light go on and knew he had to deal with the occupants. and find that document, and then deliver it. But before that he had to hide in Silver's loft, and Silver would be with him at nine. He realised that he would have to move fast.

At the same moment, D.I. Allen was reporting the latest information to Jas Singh. Allen found him still gazing at the CCTV and thought his superior was getting a little obsessed. "I have the names of the victims, Sir, Mrs. Amanda Cartwright and a Mr. David Lomax." Singh acknowledged him. "Lovers killed on the orders of a jealous spouse"? He commented dryly. "No, I don't think so. Mr. Cartwright seemed genuinely shocked, and so did Anna Sanchez, Lomax's partner, but there was one odd thing with her." "What" Singh pricked up his ears and paid closer attention. Allen went on, "Well, she looked very pale when we told her what happened; she seemed to be scared of something or someone." Singh interrupted him, "Someone, and that someone is the killer of her man." "Did she say anything else?" Singh was hoping for the positive; he did not get it. "No, she did not." Allen seemed dejected. Singh then made a decision: "I want to see her; we go tomorrow.".

Alexander looked again at his watch; it was now eight forty-five. He was hiding in the undergrowth; the light he had seen go on was now off, and the back of the house was in darkness. Alexander moved from the undergrowth and moved towards the back door; he reached it and, with his professional gentleness, opened it. He found himself standing in the kitchen in darkness.

He could hear a woman and a boy in the living room, watching television. He saw a door and went through it. He was in the hallway; the living room that was to the right now was on the left, the dining room to the left, now right. The door to the living room was closed. He put a balaclava mask on and took steps towards the door, moving quietly all the time and listening. He decided speed was of the essence. He reached the door, took a breath, and pushed his weight against it while pressing on the handle. Alexander opened the door and said in a low but stern voice, "Stay still, and no one gets hurt.".

Sarah Dawson, startled, turned round in her chair and angrily exclaimed, "Who are you? What do you want?" Alexander confronted Sarah, and Paul repeated, "Stay still, and no one gets hurt." "Are you going to shoot us? Paul had seen the gun in the hitman's hand. "No, just do as you're told, and it will be alright." The hitman looked at Paul. "Go and get your chess sets and bring them here," Alexander motioned with his gun towards the door. Go, "Paul, do as he says", Sarah instructed her son with the urgency generated by having an armed man in your home, which was obvious to the boy.

Paul wheeled out of the room and into the workroom; the other two heard him as he put the chess sets into a bag, put the bag handle around his neck, and wheeled back. The hitman was now sitting on a chair opposite Sarah, sitting on her sofa; as Paul returned, the Australian told him, "Put it on the table and go over there, "he motioned with his gun towards the opposite corner of the room. Paul went, and Alexander started opening the sets. He found what he was looking for a folded piece of paper in a white king; on it were a name, telephone number, and bank details; in short, it was the British end of the deal.

"What are you going to do with us?" Sarah Dawson put on a brave, stoic face in front of her son, hoping to show she was not scared, though she was really terrified. Alexander looked at them and thought. He considered the possibilities; he could kill them as Silver was outside waiting. He saw the headlights of Silver's car. He looked at them, staring intently. Sarah saw the blue eyes fixed on her with a hard stare as they were examining her as though with a microscope. He broke the silence: "Come with me." The Australian marching Sarah and pushing Paul took them to the hallway. "Give me your phones and turn around." The commands were snapped, and Sarah and Paul obeyed. "Don't turn around". They did not; all they heard was the door opening and footsteps hurrying out as Alexander walked quickly down the path and jumped into the passenger seat. He gave the word to Silver to drive.

Back in the house, Sarah had cautiously turned her head, and having seen that the intruder had gone, she rushed to the door to see anything. She saw nothing apart from the phones placed on the wall; the intruder had no real need of them, and Sarah thought it a funny thing that they had not been thrown away. She picked them up and returned to the house; on the way, she rang her office to report.

Silver and Alexander had driven home in silence; apart from the instruction to leave, nothing had been said. Silver drove the car into the garage, and both men got out; it was then Silver broke the silence. "Got it, and what now?" He sounded sceptical as he knew Alexander had to get out quickly. The Australian answered, "I am doing nothing; I will tell you what to do. "But I am only the contact; I know nothing," Silver interjected. "Don't worry; I tell you, then I go." Alexander turned to go into the house. "Tell your yachtsman to be ready the day after tomorrow." He did not say that two days after the meeting, the drugs would arrive.

Sarah had rung and reported the attack; 20 minutes later, two uniformed officers turned up and secured the place, and another twenty minutes later, D.I. Allen turned up.

Chapter Thirteen

"Tell me what happened, and take your time." Allen and Dawson were sitting in the kitchen. Allen had made tea, and Paul was with a female police officer. Dawson looked pale; the shock was still with her. It had arrived as soon as the uniformed unit arrived, and then she fell into the victim role. Now with Allen here, she started to try and get into detective mode. She drank her tea, took a breath, and told the story. "He came in through the back, wearing a balaclava and armed; he held us in the lounge and forced Paul to get his chess sets; then he searched through them until he found one of the white kings and unscrewed it and pulled out a piece of paper. He looked at it and then said he was leaving and took our phones and left." Allen listened intently, looked at his witness, and said, "What about him? What was he like?" Sarah Dawson thought, replying, "Big guy, about six feet four and Australian, very fit." "Sure, he was an Aussie." Allen looked concerned. "Yes, I am sure." Dawson's defiance in her voice was convincing, Allen thought. "Alright, we go from here; we put you and Paul in a hotel and search this place. I am going to ring D.S. Singh and tell him I think our serial killer got what he wanted.".

Jas Singh was about to go to sleep when the phone rang. He picked it up. "Yes, Allen," he said. He saw the other policeman's number and then the voice. "Sorry to bother you now, sir, but I think our killer has found what he was looking for." "What happened?" the senior officer suddenly perked up and listened as Allen told of the night's events. When Allen had finished, Singh told him, "Onc the crime scene people are in, I want you to come to Lomax's place. I want you there when I talk to Lomax's lady friend". I want to get the story out of her". "Yes sir, I come along; sorry to disturb you again; good night, sir." "Good night." Singh put the phone down and went off to get some sleep.

Rain poured down over the Hampshire countryside, the clouds a dark grey against a dark sky. A car was pulling up in front of a thatched cottage, one of those picture postcard cottages so beloved by tourists. Inside, Detective Superintendent Singh was giving final instructions to Detective Constable Bell and D.I. Allen. "When we see Anna Sanchez, I will do the talking and D.I. Allen, you will take notes, and when it comes to last night, you tell the story. D.C. Bell, I want you to check out the garage. If there is something here, I bet it will be in there, just the place to hide something to be moved quickly. I want to pin her down after how you described her". He looked at Allen, who nodded his agreement.

With that, the men got out of the car; Bell went off to the garage, and Allen and Singh stood at the front door. The senior officer rang the doorbell. He did not have to wait long. He heard footsteps, a female, coming towards the door. It opened, and standing before the policemen was a dark, longhaired woman with light brown skin and a face that had been ravaged in the last day by suffering bad news. "Mrs. Lomax"? "I am Anna Sanchez; we did not marry. Singh looked at her and thought he better get to business; it was better to find out while she was pliable after what Allen had said: "She looked very pale when we told her what happened; she seemed to be scared of something or someone." Watching Singh, he could see she was worried. Can we come in?" The Spaniard led the way, and everyone went into the living room. They all sat down. "How can I help you?" Anna stared at the guests, and her feelings of the expected questioning were making her feel bad. "Miss Sanchez," Singh began, "yesterday, D.I. Allen here said you looked very pale on the news of Mr. Lomax's death. Singh said, 'The inspector here seemed to think you were scared of something or someone.' We think that you know that someone, and that someone is the killer, Mr. Lomax.".

Singh had hoped that his direct approach would not frighten the woman into silence; he was lucky. Anna looked at him, tears welling up in her eyes, and she burst into tears and a savaged emotional collapse. She cried while Singh and the others looked on, then she took a deep breath and told her story":

A man named Martinez had taken Lomax to the cellar of his house and had again shown the drug stock he had. Martinez had told Lomax that Lomax, as an accountant, would be good for Martinez in Britain, washing drug money. Anna said Lomax had refused. Then Anna told the detectives that Martinez had kidnapped her without Lomax knowing and had taken her to another room, and when he went to see Lomax, Anna heard the conversation and what would happen if he did not comply. Anna then told how Martinez had her brought into the room, stripped her and strapped her to a table and raped her orally, anally, and vaginally. Lomax had seen this and had given in; Anna said Martinez had given him one hundred thousand pounds, and Lomax promised to wash the drug money.

The detectives listened, and Singh then said, "Is there anything more you want to tell us?" "What like?" replied the woman, now showing signs of stress when she guessed her man's death was a contract killing. Singh went on, "What do you know of Martinez, and do you know the killer?" "No, I don't know the killer, and Martinez is a drug dealer. David never mentioned how he met him." Anna started to cry, and the detectives decided to stop there. Just at that moment, just as they were leaving, Bell entered the house. "Can I have a word, sir? I think you should see this." " See what cried the distraught Spaniard; Singh looked at her and said, "We all go.".

Alexander had been driving since early morning. At the same time, Singh had seen Anna; the Australian had been given directions to his destination as well as using his navigator, and now he was nearly at his destination. The destination turned out to be a cottage in the middle of a wood just south of the university city of Oxford. The hitman drove up the small drive and parked behind a BMW that looked brand new. He got out of his car and went to get the chess set from the back seat; at that moment, a man appeared at the front door. He was a tall, gaunt, older-looking man, and 60, Alexander thought, and he looked unwell. Alexander spoke first. "Sir Peter Derek," "Yes," replied the gaunt man. The banker then said, "Have you got something for me from Mexico?" "Yes," Alexander showed the chess set, the older man said, "come inside." They both entered the cottage, and the banker led the way to the garden. Once there, the banker offered coffee and asked if his guest was hungry; the coffee was accepted, and the food was not. "Right down to business, let's have the set." Alexander handed it over, and Sir Peter took the white king, unscrewed the top, and took out the piece of paper. He looked at it and seemed satisfied. Alexander, watching this, was about to ask if everything was ok when the banker blurted out, "Good, ok, you have done your part; you had better go." He motioned Alexander out and said their goodbyes at the front door. Alexander got into the car, started the engine, and drove home. He had one thought, though: the other man had never asked his name.

Back at the cottage, the banker looked at the note; it was, in fact, more than a note; it was the key to the whole thing. He was to use the bank account on the paper; the account had been set up in his name. The phone number was his port contact. He now had to do two things: first, ring the contact number to confirm he had possession, and second, wait for the ship to arrive tomorrow. He poured another coffee.

Chapter Fourteen

The group was standing before the open garage door. Bell was holding a letter in his hands. He gave it to his boss, who read it. He read aloud so no one could be in any doubt as to why things had happened as they did. The letter said:

"My name is David Lomax, and this is my confession of my crimes and the organisation I work for. My employer is a Mexican drug dealer named Juan Martinez. Martinez recruited me after showing me his business in the cellar of his house and abusing my girlfriend, Anna, in front of me. I gave in, and he made me launder drug profits through the firm of accountants I work for. The name of the company was Hernandez Holdings, San Antonio, USA. In spring this year, I had a visit from Mr Cardenas, an associate of Martinez, who told me of a plan to import the largest quantity of cocaine ever attempted into the UK; it was on board the SS Sea Giant, coming to Southampton on 21st March 2024. I also stuck the envelope under a windscreen wiper on a police car, confirming SS Sea Giant as the ship "Halbury" as my home and "Chess Piece" to give a clue about the information. I was told I would receive directions to contact here in the UK and to bring certain information to him. I was told not to do anything until this information was received; I was later told the information would be sealed in the inside of a chess piece, a white king. I was to give this to my son, and then under the cover of the chess tournament, I was to take the set home, open the king, and deal with the information." Singh took a breath and said, "This is now the important part." He continued to read.

"However, my son had a collision accident with a boy in a wheelchair. I learnt this boy's name was Dawson and where he lived. I tried to recover the set but failed. At this point, Martinez sent a man called Alexander to do the job I was meant to do. I think he is going to kill me. He is Australian. I don't know what is to happen or what to do; if I die, I leave this as a contribution to catching my killer".

Singh stopped reading, took another breath, and said, "Right, this is our plan, D. I, Allen, get this name out with his picture and make it clear he is wanted for three murders. Now we have a name; we have a chance. Also, find out where he came in and where he was before he got here.

Singh turned to D.C. Bell, "You and I are going to Southampton; that ship is going to be in Southampton the day after tomorrow." Finally, he turned to Anna, "I'd like to see the bank account, please." Anna took him inside, picked up her phone, and opened the online banking app. Singh looked at it; his eyes told him that Lomax and his family were the owners of exactly two million pounds as of today.

Singh pondered and said, "You kept all this and did not spend?" Anna nodded, "David wanted it that way; no one must know. We could have moved out of here years ago, but David said no.".

She then said, "What will happen to me?" Singh looked and thought. He honestly did not know he could not charge her; she had committed no crime but had been a victim of a crime, a sex crime. She had not hindered the investigation as such; in fact, the only thing she was guilty of was having knowledge of David Lomax and his laundering activity, and even then had not taken part. Singh stared into space; he looked at Bell and then again at Anna; finally, he said, "We have to see.".

It was 12:30 pm, and the rain that had greeted the detectives was now paying a visit to Drayford. As usual, for it was a Wednesday, Tommy Silver was sitting at his desk and doing his books, or rather sharing the Value Added Tax Money between himself and the British Government; Tommy thought that VAT was stifling his business. Therefore, he needed more than the current government. He had sent Alexander off that morning with his best sports car to see the contact. Now he was waiting for the Australian because he had to tell the man he was going abroad later tonight. It had been a difficult conversation with the yacht owner, his brother Andy Silver. Andy was like his brother, a small man with small features. He was sixty; his brother was fifty-eight, and he too had iron-grey hair, the thin build, but with piercing blue eyes, from mother and not the grey from father.

Tommy cast his mind back to the phone call and the fight that had developed when Andy had told him that he, Andy, had worked out who his passenger was and was not happy. Tommy remembered the conversation: "What the fuck? Why should I do that? I am not taking psychos on board," "Andy, why not? You smuggled people, and it's good money", "I don't bloody care." "Why not? You agreed to it," Tommy seemed slightly off balance by his brother's words; his brother carried on. "That was before the police got his picture and name; now it is all over the place. Just put the television or radio on.".

Tommy had and found it was true: the face and name were there for the world to see. Tommy saw no alternative but to move as soon as the Australian was back. He spoke to Andy, "Listen, if you do this for me, I throw in an extra ten thousand just for you." "Ten thousand," his brother seemed stunned. "Yes, you have the money tonight in your account." There was silence on the phone, then Andy answered, "Agreed, I will do it. See you tonight." Tommy gave his thanks, put the phone down, and breathed a sigh of relief. Twenty minutes later, while he was depriving the government of its legal tax requirement, he heard a car pull up.

He moved from his desk and looked out the window; it was the hitman. Silver went to meet him just outside the repair bay door. "Job done." Silver made small talk. "Yes, but the police know about me; we have to go." Alexander looked at the other man and waited for a reply. "Yes, we are going tonight. I just shut up the garage, and then we go, first to get your stuff and then to Cornwall." Tommy Silver was already making his way back inside to lock up, leaving Alexander to change cars and wait.

He did not have to wait long. Silver soon returned, got in the car, started the engine, and they were off. Silver had on his mind how to hide a six-foot-two Australian from the police while on the move; he watched his passenger. The passenger looked straight ahead and said nothing.

Soon, they got there, and Alexander went to get his stuff. Silver wrote a note for Thresa, his girlfriend, grabbed some food and drink, and headed back to the car. Robert Alexander reappeared with his case and a bag, threw them in the boot, and got back in the car. "Ready?" Silver asked awkwardly. The Australian just nodded. Next stop: Cornwall.

"We are going to take the long way round," Silver talked as they drove, "plenty of A roads and away from motorway patrols." The Australian listened and just said, "Alright", "we will be there out 6 pm." " Silver followed up. The passenger said nothing.

Jas Singh had been busy; he had made sure that the name and photograph had been sent out together. He called London and spoken to Smith; Smith had promised to check files and talk to contacts he had. Singh had congratulated D.I. Allen for his work, and now it was time to wait for a sighting or information.

He then had also thought about Anna; he had to write a report and send it to the Crown Prosecution Service, or CPS, to deal with it; he could imagine they could use one of their favourite terms, either "not in the public interest" or "insufficient evidence." He would leave it at that; that's all.

CHAPTER FIFTEEN

They had been driving for twenty minutes when suddenly, as they were going past the car park behind the Dawson house, the hitman shouted, "Stop." Silver smashed his foot against the brake pedal, and the car screeched to a halt as the tires desperately gripped the road, keeping it from flying off the road. "What's the matter? Why do you want to stop?" Tommy fired the questions rapidly; the Australian looked at him directly in the eye. "Wait" was his only word.

Silver watched as the passenger got out and ran across the road, disappearing into the car park. He wondered what was going on.

In the car park, Alexander looked around; there was no one else; he was alone, and he could not see the car, and Tommy could not see him. He felt satisfied. He walked towards the public toilet at the far end of the car park, went behind to the small picnic area, and, kneeling down, began digging. Soon he recovered the objects he wanted. First, a Heckler and Koch P30 handgun with ammunition; second, a combat knife, a Fairbairn Sykes fighting knife; and finally, money and a credit card, all three wrapped in plastic and ready for his flight. He was pleased with himself; it had been a good idea. He had rung the banker on the way home and told him what he wanted, the parcels, and where to get them. He had then rung an old friend in Oxford, a Charlie Boyer. They had met in Afghanistan, Boyer a Marine Commando and Alexander as an Australian soldier. They had kept in touch, and Boyer had left the Marines and tried civilian life; it had not worked, and Boyer had fallen into hard times until a friend had suggested crime. Boyer agreed and soon found himself a niche supplying weapons, ammunition, and money to the underworld as a fixer. He had stayed in touch with the hitman; Alexander had promised himself to use Bowyer; now that time had come, hence the banker burying this gear early that morning and Alexander now recovering it.

He went back to the car; Tommy saw him and called out, "Got it, whatever it was." Tommy was ignored. The Australian just looked, looked him in the eye, Silver started the car, and off they went.

Detective Chief Inspector Daniel Smith was depressed; the morning had been bad—no, it had been terrible. First, his girlfriend, the lawyer, had been offered a promotion and a new position in New York; she had accepted and told Smith he could come if he wanted. He had said no, and the lawyer, being a lawyer, had ended their relationship that morning, adding she was an independent woman and, being so, was taking one of the firm's male partners with her instead of the policeman.

But that was not all; soon after, M.I. 5, disguised as a man calling himself Harrison, no forename, turned up with Detective Chief Superintendent Alan Cartwright in tow. Both men were looking at Smith for answers. Harrison started the ball rolling, "When the bloody hell did you get this photograph, and why were we not informed of Robert Alexander's presence in the UK?" Smith retorted with venom, "A witness took it, and we believe this is a criminal matter, not state security.".

"Is that so? Well, your man is more than just a criminal. Tell him, Cartwright.". Cartwright was reading from a file; he looked at Harrison and the Smiths, "You had better read this." Cartwright handed Smith the file, and Smith opened it and started to read. He read the first page and then stopped and looked surprised. He said to Harrison, "I see he is everywhere." "Yes, he is a right world traveller, a killer of politicians, criminals, and police, and he is here, and you did not make it known." "As I said, we thought it was a criminal investigation." Smith stuck to his guns. Cartwright intervened. "I think we should all take a breath; I promise we will pass any information on when available. He looked at M.I.5; Harrison agreed and also gave an apology for his outburst. Smith reciprocated, and with that, Harrison took the file and left.

"What was that really all about?" Smith was thinking aloud. "Well, you read the file on the suspected killer, no face and no name, only bits to go on until now, the invisible man. Now we have a chance to catch him, and with him killing your cleaning lady, we have a real chance. You are the only one in the world who knows this man." But how did Harrison guess or think it was the man they wanted"?

Cartwright thought, then answered. "He recently came back from Germany after having killed a Turkish gangster who had refused to pay his boss one Martinez. Unfortunately, he kicked off a drug war in Hamburg that killed fifty people; fifteen were kids on a school bus when one of the gangs decided to kill the son of a drug dealer. Unfortunately, to make sure they did the job, they took fourteen others with the target. When the German police investigated, the only thing found was a witness who described a tattoo on the inside of the right hand. "So not many people have that," Smith looked perplexed. "They could have caught him." "No, someone shot the witness before he could talk properly, gunned down in a police station, bit of a balls-up actually, and more so as he slipped through the net here, probably wearing gloves when he got here; it is only your teenager who got the first shot of him in the world."

"I see." Smith grinned at the thought he was responsible for closing in on the mystery man. "Think you could find him?" Cartwright's question left Smith on the spot. "Well, we've been given the greatest chance ever, apparently, and we must lose it." Cartwright said nothing, just grinned, but was interrupted when the phone rang.

Smith answered the phone. "Detective Chief Inspector Daniel Smith speaking." "Dan, is Jas listening? We lost Alexander, but we can find him, and also, I am going down to the docks tomorrow; the drugs are on the way." Smith was excited. "If he comes this way, we will grab him." "OK", Dan, if we find him, we let you now." The Hampshire detective smiled to himself at the informality and friendship they had struck up.

Jas had put the phone down when D.C. Bell appeared in the office. "Nothing yet, sir, all quiet," Jas thought. He looked at the clock on the wall, three in the afternoon, two and a half hours, and not even a time waster to get things going. He looked at Bell, who waited for an answer; he got it: "We need a miracle, Bell, a miracle.".

Theresa Moore returned home with shopping. She parked the car, got out, walked up the pathway, and opened the shouting, "Tommy, I'm home. Need help with shopping?" There was silence. Theresa went in, looked around, and saw no sign of Tommy or, for that matter, their guest. Theresa looked around; the place was in a mess. She cursed Tommy; he had not tidied up. She was about to go when she found the note. She cursed Tommy again; she thought about the shopping: nothing for the freezer, so she decided to make herself a coffee; after all, if Tommy could be lazy, so could she. She turned the radio on for the company, just in time for the three o'clock news; she heard, "Police are looking for Robert Alexander a....." Theresa's blood ran cold. She had seen the guest, was not meant to have seen him because Tommy had not told her and did not think she knew, but she did, and she was frightened; she thought of Tommy: Was he already dead? Was he on the run for murder? Her mind spun and spun. She really had no idea of what to do. She then had a light bulb moment; the one thing Tommy had told her never to do under any circumstances. But this time she had to for Tommy, whatever had happened. She picked up the phone and called the police.

"Hampshire Police, how can I help today?" the shrill operator's voice floated down the line. "I like to speak to the detective leading the hunt for Robert Alexander.".

CHAPTER SIXTEEN

"Just a minute, caller," the voice continued, "just put you through." A minute later, Thresa heard a male voice, "Detective Inspector Peter Allen speaking. "Are you leading the hunt for Robert Lexander?" "No, but I am part of the team; tell me what you know." "We had him here in our loft; he is gone with my Tommy. I'm ever so worried." "Ok, calm down, tell me your name and then Tommy's surname." "I am Thresa Moore and Tommy's surname is Silver."

Allen tensed; he thought for a second and then asked, "Is that Tommy Silver of Silvers Garage in Drayford?" "Yes, it is." Allen grabbed a notepad and began to scribble the beginnings of a note for Singh. He spoke again. "Do you know how long they have been gone?" "no" came the reply. "How did they go?" Allen pressed quickly, "They took Tommy's car; it is a blue BMW 2 registration HA01HAC."

Theresa rambled about the information; such was the panic over what was going to happen to Tommy. She blurted out, "I know Tommy's not a good guy, but he doesn't deserve this." Allen said nothing to that but told Thresa, "I am sending a detective to you to look around; they will be with you soon. Thank you for the information; it will all be alright. Okay, I will wait here." Thresa was feeling ill with the thought of her dead Tommy. Allen put the phone down and dialled a number. Detective Sergeant Fiona Macpherson answered, and Allen told her what was going on and what he wanted her to do. Then, he had the car number plate sent out to all patrols and to other police forces. He then went upstairs to see if Singh had finished with his press briefing.

As he went up the stairs, he went past a clock. It said twenty-to-four in the afternoon.

"I'm feeling hungry; I haven't eaten since breakfast." Silver felt his empty stomach; they had been driving for about two and a half hours, made good time, and had no problems. Silver reflected on the ease of the trip. The hitman said nothing but just looked ahead. "Look, there is a pub down the road. I know it; we can stop there." Silver waited for an answer; the passenger looked and just nodded his agreement.

They drove into the car park of the "Wayside Inn." Alexander looked at the place, another postcard picture from England, he thought. Silver parked the car, and both men got out. It was a bright day, and Silver sat down at a table near the entrance. Soon, a waitress came out; the hitman looked at her. Middle Eastern, he guessed, probably from a boat that was not stopped, as everybody seemed to want to get to the UK; he found the irony of him trying to get out amusing. Silver broke his thought.

"The chicken salad is good, and they brew their own beer." Alexander looked at him and the waitress; he addressed her with, "Same for me then." They waited for their food. The Australian finally became talkative, "If we eat now, we will be late for the contact." "No, my contact has said he could sail on the morning tide; staying on board one night is okay, and no one will find you, I've been assured. Alexander was about to say something when a glint caught his eye.

Alexander Focused his eyes; the glint became a car, a car with markings, and the word "Police." He tensed; so did

Silver. Both men watched as two police officers got out, one a constable, the other a woman, very pretty, thought the hitman; then he saw the three stripes of a police sergeant, and coming out of his erotic thought over the blonde woman before him, he remembered she is the enemy. "What do we do? "Silvers's voice sounded stressed. "Nothing," said the Australian; he followed up. "Stay cool, and we'll wait.".

The two men stayed seated and watched as the two police officers went into the pub; at the same time, the waitress came out with the food and drink for Silver and Alexander. Silver quickly asked, "What's going on?" The waitress hesitated to think an admission would get her sacked. However, she felt it was a small thing and replied, "There was a fight last night here in the carpark. The police are still checking details". Silver looked visibly happy; the hitman said and did absolutely nothing, just stared at the police car, deep in thought...

The police came back out and walked back to their car. The hitman watched Silver eat and drink. The officers reached their car, and when the sergeant stopped and answered her radio, they were too far away to hear what was being said, but, watching, Alexander knew. He watched, and sure enough, his thoughts were confirmed; the two officers looked at the blue BMW 2 registration HA01HAC, and they started walking towards Silver's car. "What the hell now?" Silver was audibly panicking. "Stop eating and drinking; we are going." Alexander got to his feet and moved towards the standing police officers. They saw him. "Is this your car, sir?" The woman sergeant looked at the hitman, who, sensing she was examining her arrest options because he was far bigger than she was, only said, "No.". "Is it your car, sir?" the sergeant addressed Silver, who tried to answer but could not because Alexander had, at that moment, exploded into action.

He had gotten very close to the constable, and now only standing a foot away, he lunged for him and kneed the constable in the groin; the man doubled up, and then Alexander pulled his head up, exposing his throat, and with a clenched fist smashed the policeman in the throat. The policewoman lunged with her baton, trying to subdue the hitman. She swung the baton to try and catch his legs, but he was too fast, and the baton entered empty space. The woman looked up, and there was no one in front of her; then she felt arms encircle her and push her up against the police car, for Alexander had got behind her and was now using all his weight and strength. She fought and struggled, but the hitman squeezed her tightly; then, as witnesses all two of them described later, there were two flashes of light in the afternoon sun and screams. Then the policewoman fell to the floor face down, and a stream of blood flowed from under her across the car park.

Alexander was standing over her bloodied knife in hand. He looked at the bodies, then calmly wiped the blade clean on the dying sergeant's uniform.

While all this had been going on, Silver had been holding on to his car as though it was a shield against the vengeful Australian; his mind was rushing while his eyes processed the slaughter that was before him, and his stomach had a nauseous feeling. He had never liked the hitman, and now it was more than dislike; now it was cold-blooded fear. He was about to open his mouth when the hitman grabbed him and pushed him into the passenger seat, shouting, "I will drive." He then got in, started the car, and they were off. They pulled onto the road; Alexander growled again. "How long do we get there, and what time are we leaving tomorrow?" Silver rattled his answers off: "About two hours, maybe two and a half; you're leaving six minutes past three tomorrow morning," he added, "Why the bloody hell did you kill those two?" He did not give a response, Alexander staring straight ahead and cut off from humanity.

Back at the "Wayside" Inn, there was chaos; the two witnesses, the waitress and a customer raised the alarm. Soon, the police and an ambulance arrived; somebody had covered the dead, and the two officers took statements. It had happened all very fast, the waitress said, and the customer agreed and also commented on the speed of the police reaction.

The officers finished taking statements when the crime scene unit turned up, and in pursuit were two detectives. The senior of the two uniformed officers saw the white car and said to the younger, ", "Bob" was about to ask who Saunders was when a giant Scotsman got out of the car, followed by a man who was not a giant. "Afternoon, Paul" the Scotsman greeted the senior officer. "What you got here?" Saunders learnt what was known and then said, "Alright, I see the witnesses." Saunders first saw the waitress. "I'm Detective Inspector Saunders; this is Detective Sergeant James. You are?" The waitress answered, "Sofia." "Ok, tell me again what you saw." So, Sofia did, and the detective listened and finally said thank you.

It was then James took a phone call; he listened and then turned to his superior: "It's for you, sir." "Saunders speaking," the Scotsman sounded gruff as he did not like being disturbed during interviewing, even though he had finished only with the first witness. He intently held the phone to his ear as the voice beyond told him all about the Southampton alert. He responded with, "Alright when I get back, I think I need a Zoom meeting with this Singh.

In Southampton, Singh had been busy organising the Zoom; there were to be three,

Singh, Smith, and Saunders, and the topic was the hitman; as for the ship, that was now a side issue; the Australian had to be caught. He thought about his target: Where was he now? What was he doing?

Chapter Seventeen

At that moment, the target was nearly at his objective, only thirty minutes away. During the trip there had been silence; no one had spoken, the Australian not needing to speak, Silver being in pure terror after what he had seen and wondering if he was next. He was thinking when the hitman said, "Look." Silver looked, and he noticed they were on the A390, and he could see the river Fowey. "We're nearly there, just into Fowey; head for the river, and we will find our contact." They drove on into town, finally finding Fore Street and driving towards the harbour. "There is the Harbour fice." Silver pointed out the car park, "We can park in there." The Australian took the car to the carpark, parked up, and the two got out and went to the Albert Jetty.

"Well gentlemen, glad you could come," Singh looked at his screen and saw the youngish face of the forty-year-old Smith from London and the oldish face of the forty-something Scotsman from Cornwall. Singh continued: "Well, here it is, gentlemen: our target has now killed five people and is believed to be in Cornwall. Well, "if he appears in London, we'll get him." Smith interjected, "He won't growl at the Scotsman; he is getting out through Cornwall, and soon enough will find the car again, and then him." He added, "If he is planning to go back to London from here, he is taking a hell of a risk; he would get caught sooner or later; we know too much." Saunders could have added that Cornwall's infrastructure being like it was meant that fast escape would be difficult, as the only main roads were the A38 and A30, limiting choice for a man on the run. Singh then told them about Lomax's "Last Testament and Confession" and also the drug shipment. Smith said he would come down tonight as he wanted to be involved; Saunders promised again to find the killer. "Ok gentlemen, let's get to it." With that, Singh ended the meeting.

"Did you get that message out to the harbour master's along the south oast?" "Yes sir, as you asked. ""You did Fowey rst." "Yes, sir." "Good." Saunders smiled to himself; on the way back from Wayside Inn, he had looked at an Ordinance Survey map. He found the Wayside Inn and noticed that it was directly between Polperro and Fowey. The target had left and driven toward Fowey; he could have turned back and gone for Polperro, Saunders thought, but it was unlikely. Fowey was the destination because, as Saunders guessed, they had a contact, so Saunders had warned the Fowey harbour master...

The spring weather had changed, having driven in sunlight and spring warmth; Alexander and Silver now stood on the Albert Jetty in a chill wind, the clouds turning grey. Silver was sending a WhatsApp message; he sent it, and soon, a reply came as his phone sang its whistling tune. Silver read the message and told the waiting Alexander, "Our man is coming ashore." "Why can't we go to him?" Alexander tensed at the thought of treachery; Silver thought of being killed if things went wrong. Silver answered:

"That's the way it is to be; that was what was agreed." The Australian tensed and made his fists into balls. Tommy Silver said, "Calm down; it will be alright." Alexander just stared.

While Alexander was staring, saying nothing, in the Harbour Office, Harry Burton, Fowey Harbour Master, was talking to Mike Jarvis, a boat owner, over harbour charges and, in between, venting his spleen at the request from the police. "I knew it, that killer, the Australian they're after, and they want me to keep a lookout for the car, and what I am to do when I find the car, and he finds me." "Well, you can only report what you see," Jarvis looked at the Harbour Master, who obviously did not like the idea of a killer in his midst. Burton rambled on, and you know what? They have sent me a description of a blue BMW 2 registration HA01HAC. What makes them think it is here in Fowey, especially in the car park? Jarvis was about to answer when the door opened. It was Harry Burton's children, Lucy and James. "Hi Dad, Mum asked us to come with this. They handed a lunch box over, Harry realising he had left it at home; he looked at the children. "Aren't you two meant to be in school?" "School's over, Dad. We are just going to the park; we were to drop your supper on the way." Lucy explained. Harry thought about this and said, "Thanks." He also thought his daughter was just like her mother, organised, efficient, and always remembering others. He turned to his son, who was car mad. "How's that model of the Jaguar E-type coming on?" "Coming on fine, Dad," he added, "there is a blue BMW 2 in the car park, stunning." Harry's smile that was on his face suddenly vanished. He went over to the window, looked out, and saw the car. "Yes, it is Jim. "Now you two get to the park." The children left, and as soon as Burton saw the door close, he picked up the phone and asked to speak to whoever was in charge of the case regarding the BMW.

Tommy Silver and Robert Alexander were still waiting. It had been about twenty minutes, and no one had appeared yet. Alexander, tense and glaring at the other man, snapped in an aggressive tone,

"Where is he? Send another WhatsApp."

Silver pulled the phone out of his pocket but then paused, looking out toward the river. A man in a rowing boat was approaching them. Soon, the boat arrived at the jetty, and Tommy's face lit up.

"Well, better late than never," he said, hugging his brother, Andy.

Alexander watched the reunion with a casual look. Tommy gestured toward the newcomer and introduced him.

"This is my brother, Andy."

Tommy hoped this information would reassure Alexander, his hitman, that everything was still under control and "in the family." Alexander gave a curt,

"Hello."

Andy Silver nodded and replied, "Hello." Then, turning to Tommy, he said,

"We're all set. We're going tomorrow on the tide. Just get the guest into the boat here, and then we'll board the yacht and rest up. Tomorrow, we leave."

Andy paused and asked,

"Nothing left to chance, right?"

Before Tommy could answer, Alexander interrupted,

"Tell him."

Andy frowned,

"Tell me what?"

The words had barely left his mouth when a sharp pain shot through his stomach. He clutched at his middle, realizing too late something was wrong. Before Tommy could explain, the truth spilt out in the worst way possible.

Andy looked at his brother, his expression a mix of anger and betrayal.

"Why didn't you get rid of the bloody car?"

Tommy froze, looking stunned. He knew he should have taken care of it, but his fear of what he'd seen—and of the hitman—had paralyzed him.

"Sorry, Andy," he stammered. "But we needed the car. I thought it wouldn't matter."

Andy could see the fear in his brother's eyes, fear not of him but of the Australian hitman. Taking a deep breath to steady himself, Andy asked,

"Alright. Where is the car now?"

Tommy hesitated. "It's in the car park, and… it still has stuff in it."

Andy's eyes narrowed. Tommy was clearly worried the car might have been seen. Andy nodded sharply.

"Okay. We go back and get the stuff," he said firmly, taking the lead.

CHAPTER EIGHTEEN

"Devon and Cornwall Police, the operators, firm voice a male, brought Burton to attention from the worry he had suffered. "I found the car in the hunt for the suspect in the Hampshire killings." The operator remained calm. "Yes, I just put you through." Burton listened as some classical music played; he was not sure what it was, but it did not really matter; he heard a Scottish voice, "Detective"

Inspector Robert Saunders, you have found the car, Mr. ... "Burton, Harold Burton, I am the Harbour Master at Fowey." "Where did you find the car?" "In our carpark." "It is the same car." Burton thought for a moment and confirmed it was so.

Saunders thought for a moment. He then fired questions and suggestions: "Have you seen the occupants?" "No". "Do you know where they could be going? Has anyone told you when they are having?" Burton thought and said, "No, I don't know where they are going, and I have three vessels leaving, two early tomorrow and one late tomorrow." "How early, "Saunders's voice suddenly gained an urgency. "Six minutes past three in the morning." Burton rattled off the details. Saunders asked if he could have the details, and Burton agreed, and Saunders made plans to pass the information on.

Saunders was ending the conversation with Burton, who was about to put the phone down, when he looked out of the window and saw three men. "I can see them; they are around the car," "The BMW," asked Saunders. "Yes, one tall and two short," Burton gave descriptions of all three, Saunders made a note, the Australian, the other driver, and a third unknown man. Saunders thought and placed his thought into words. "You know the other man," "Yes. ""He is an owner here; his name is Andrew Silver; we know him as Andy." Saunders was stunned; he knew of Tommy Silver, and now there was an Andy Silver. The detective spoke with a firm urgency in his voice. "Mr. Burton, keep an eye on the car, and Mr. Silvers, the boat; please tell us if anything happens. "Ok," said Burton, feeling very unhappy he was playing spy to a killer.

Saunders, having finished with Burton, called his sergeant and got him to disperse the information; he then dialled a number, and soon Jasleen Singh's voice came over the phone. Saunders wasted no time and got to the point about the Silver Brothers, Singh confirmed, and Saunders then thought aloud: "Alexander is going by boat, which is provided by Andrew Silver, Tommy Silver having arranged it, there leaving six minutes past three tomorrow morning on the tide." "Ok, so do we have any idea on how to stop them? It is already eight thirty in the evening." Singh was thinking hard, and realising that the Australian was maybe going to slip through their fingers, he had decided to act now. Saunders also came to that conclusion, and both detectives decided the boat had to be stopped. Saunders promised he would talk to the harbour master.

"Got everything," Andy Silver had watched as the Australian emptied the car of his worldly possessions: a rucksack and a cotton carrier bag. Tommy had just watched and said nothing. His fear of Alexander growing by the minute. "Now to get rid of the car, got any petrol to burn it out?" Andy gave a precise instruction in a business voice.

"No," said Tommy, his voice getting lower as he would be the one to dispose of the car. Andy looked at his brother with a stern look of someone dealing with an idiot. "Ok, listen, take the car and leave town. As you leave town, there is a public area in the woods; drive into it but don't stop there. There is a cart track; drive down it until you come to a bungalow. Here are the keys to the garage; lock the car in the garage." " Who lives there? Tommy did not like the idea; he thought it more trouble. "I live there, but because of your friend here, I may not be able to come home for a bit of time." "How long?" Tommy was surprised. "I don't know; perhaps I won't return. For a second Tommy thought he saw a tear, a hint of sadness; he went on, "But you stay in touch." Andy did not say anything; he just smiled and motioned towards the car, and then he and the hitman headed for the jetty and the rowing boat. The time was nine o'clock.

At the same time Singh was preparing to talk to Mary James, senior customs officer at Southampton, he was still waiting for Saunders to ring back about catching the killer. Saunders had stayed silent, so he dialled the number of customs in outhampton.

He listened for the ringtone, and soon a well-trained and professional voice answered, "Mary James, HMRC". Detective Superintendent Singh, Singh replied, "Oh yes, I was warned that you wanted to talk to me about the SS Sea Giant." "Yes, she is arriving tomorrow." Singh, we need to board her; we have good intelligence she has drugs aboard. "Yes, I am aware of the case. One of your colleagues, a man called Smith, was here earlier this month. By the way, the ship docks tomorrow at seven thirty-five in the morning at high tide". Mary James was reading from a file that Singh could not see. "Can get on board as soon as she docks." "We can. I take it the drugs are in a container," James asked the obvious. "It is, and we think it may be two containers." "I see," said James. "Well, see you tomorrow morning at seven am. Don't be late; I have my team already." Singh wished her good night.

Mary James put the phone down and looked at the man sitting opposite, who had been called in to hear the conversation. "Well, Ben, we go tomorrow, and we do a full search." "Yes, ma'am, and do you think we will find anything?" "Yes," it was a simple, plain answer; the questioner did not push the subject. "Good night, Ben. See you tomorrow." Mary James got up to leave. "Good night, ma'am".

Her deputy opened the door, and she went through to her home. Ben had a phone call to make, and it was urgent.

At the same time another meeting was ending, Saunders had telephoned the harbour master again, asking about how best to arrest someone on a boat without giving warning. Burton had told him that anyone who was suspected of a crime could be so arrested; he also mentioned it was better to intercept the boat while it was moving.

Saunders then had a thought: they were leaving on high tide; could they be intercepted further down the river by boat? Burton said it was possible because the channel was narrow, and that meant there would be little chance of manoeuvre, and then Andy Silver had had no chance of getting away. Saunders then made his plan. Burton agreed, and tomorrow at four, all would be ready.

Ben was making his phone call. He had been given a phone number in case of trouble, for he had the responsibility of making sure the two containers with the drugs got through customs; after all, that was what his employers, the Mexicans, wanted, and they had paid him well. They also threatened him well. He had been sent a video of a woman being raped and a frightened Englishman agreeing to work for the cartel. A note with it also informed him they knew his house and his wife. To prove the point, for about a month two men had sat outside his house telling him they were watching what he was doing and when his wife was alone. Benjamin Williams, for that was his name, had agreed to work for them. He remembered the first contact: two men had appeared early in March. They had proposed he work for them. They told him they knew about the gambling debts, that his wife did not, and they could help. That's when the threats started.

He listened to the ringtone finally a recorded message appeared. He left the message in plain language asking for help, saying, "It's Ben. I need help. I am going to be discovered. I don't know what to do about the stuff. But help would never come. It was Tommy Silvers, phone, his voice, his message: help would never come.

CHAPTER NINETEEN

The Casa Dorada Acapulco

Antonio Cardenas stood on the beach looking at the waves as they rose from the Pacific and gently crawled up the shore. It had been days since Alexander had spoken, and his boss, Juan Martinez, had moved into the little bungalow that was built for the visitors. He had not been seen or heard of since. In the days gone by, Cardenas had only seen two visitors.

One was a police chief, and the other was an unknown man. The first visit had ended quickly, but the second had stayed two days and left. But Martinez had not emerged from his exile. Cardenas continued his watching when he sensed someone behind him; he spun around and was confronted by Martinez. Cardenas looked at him; he had aged, he looked tired, and he had a blank look. Cardenas was about to say "hello" when Martinez cut him off: "It's over, all over, no deal, no money, all gone."

Cardenas asked him why. Martinez explained his two visitors: the police chief gave him information that the British had requested, someone had blown Alexander wide open, and now he was on the run. The second visitor had been Miguel, the shadow, or Sombra in Spanish. Cardenas knew him; he was the cartel lawyer, the face of the cartel; he was also the fixer, travelling around the world fixing things for Martinez. Apart from the current deal, Martinez had sent Cardenas to London; so secret and important was the shipment that even Miguel must not be allowed a whiff of what was going on.

Cardenas asked the question, "What was with Miguel?" Martinez told his underling, "Miguel did some work for me; the police are closing in on Alexander. Martinez's voice began to rise; he was angry. You remember you said he may not pull the thing g off. Well, thanks to Lomax, the entire thing is dead; he wrote a confession before he was killed. "How do you know?" "Miguel found out from the police chief that the British sent all they had on Alexander". He is of no longer use to me or the artel." So, what now? "Cardenas looked perplexed. "Alexander is on his own; no more help and he will no longer be welcome. He has to learn to stay away; eventually, it will kill him." Martinez turned to go back to the house. "Want some lunch? Come on, I'm hungry, he told the still perplexed Cardenas. Martinez then said something never heard before: Martinez suddenly piped up. "I apologise; I should have listened to you; to quote you, "'He has failed." "I have failed." "We all failed," the two men walked up the steps to the Casa Dorada. The time in Mexico was six in the evening, 1 am in Britain.

Detective Constable David Willis looked through his binoculars. He was in the office of the harbour master; the time was one fifteen in the morning. His target was the Lucky Lady, Andy.

Silvers boat, he came on shift at midnight, and so far nothing, nothing at all. He looked again at the yacht, a 35 ft steel gaff cutter with a lifting keel and a red hull. He did not know anything about sailing or boats, but this one looked nice; he wondered just how much had been paid.

The door opened; Saunders wandered in. "Anything." "No sir, nothing. They went on board, and that was that." Saunders picked up the binoculars. "Nice boat," he said. He also liked what he saw. "Keep your eyes open; as soon as he moves, tell us." With that, Saunders left the room and Willis to his lonely vigil.

The Casa Dorada Acapulco

Antonio Cardenas sat in the dining room; he was alone, Martinez having disappeared without a word. He looked out at the sea and the beach through the window that took up virtually the entire wall. He helped himself to wine; he thought about what was happening now. Martinez reappeared; he had a file under his arm. "I am going to deal with Alexander; I am going to hand him over to the Germans.

Remember that gang war that broke out in Germany?" Cardenas nodded. "Well, I think they should have him in custody, terrorist he is." "But he will talk," Cardenas thought aloud. "No, he won't." Martinez smiled. "He will know who betrayed him; he will also know that we can reach him anytime, any place." "Yes, that is why he will talk." Cardenas had no grasp of his boss's thought. Martinez saw the confusion in his man's eyes and spoke. "Firstly, Miguel, Will travel to Mexico City and make sure this file gets to the German embassy. Second, the Germans will hunt and find Alexander; Alexander will fight his way out, and when captured, he will go on the run. Then we or they kill him; that way they kill a terrorist, and we kill our man. They won't know about the cartel from him. "But what if he surrenders?

"Cardenas tried to make his boss see sense in what a mad scheme it was.

"He will fight his way out for his freedom; no one will be allowed to get in the way. We know that, don't we?" Cardenas thought for a moment. Then he remembered Los Angeles; Alexander had been caught on the tenth floor of an office block belonging to a Colombian. The Colombian had sent six of his men to deal with Alexander; three had been shot, two stabbed, and the sixth was sent to the ground floor without using the lift. Yes, Cardenas thought, Alexander would fight his way out. Cardenas was still pondering the coming bloodbath in Britain when he noticed that Martinez was on the phone setting the plan in motion.

In Cornwall, it was two thirty in the morning. Willis still had one and a half hours before his shift ended, and so far, he had seen nothing, nothing until now. Two men were on deck, a short man and a tall man; that was the Australian. Willis opened his radio: "O.P. 1 to base, O.P. 1 to base, the tourists are moving." "Base to O.P. 1 Base to O.P. 1, what is happening?" Saunders remained calm and waited for the response. "They are getting ready to leave and drinking coffee, a lot of activity.".

"Alright, Willis, keep me informed. Out." Saunders looked at the group in the van. There were three others: the Harbour Master, the Superintendent Commander for the area, and a firearms officer, an inspector. It was the inspector who spoke first: "Are there firearms?" Saunders replied immediately, "Yes, definitely. "Have you seen hem?" The inspector was nothing if not persistent. "We believe he is armed; we have nothing to the contrary." Saunders looked at the officer, who settled for the best answer he was going to get. Saunders also pondered the question he could have told the inspector that five people were already dead, and the Australian had his body; yes, he was dangerous.

On board the Lucky Lady, Andy was sharing out more coffee. He had, in the short time, been told his guest's name or asked; in fact, his guest had hardly spoken. "Just finish this, and then I get the engine going." Andy had hoped this would start a conversation; the Australian just nodded. Andy finished his coffee. "Going below, we will be finished soon. "With that, Andy went below, leaving Alexander looking out to sea. He could hear the noise of coverings being taken, switches and buttons being pushed, and soon the humming and thumping noise of a boat engine.

Alexander listened and watched. He was watching for trouble, as he always did, as a second-nature safety precaution. He scanned the horizon; there were plenty of lights on, and he could see quite far. He scanned the horizon right to the left and left to right and then from the left again. It was this second sweep he saw it. A mass of lights, slowly moving towards them, made Alexander tense. At that moment, Andy reappeared and was surprised to hear the Australian who asked, "What do you think that is?" "Maybe the lifeboat is out on a rescue or training, but it's early," Andy told him and looked at his watch as well; it said three thirty. "We best get underway," Andy began to get the anchor up. Alexander was not listening; he was now alert, watching the approaching boat, with a tension and feeling of trouble coming.

CHAPTER TWENTY

The tension got worse; the boat was coming closer. "Get the boat moving and try and stay out of sight." Alexander barked the order to Andy, who obeyed without a murmur. Alexander then took cover and a tarpaulin, the gun tucked into his belt, now cocked and ready, the knife strapped to his leg. He waited as the boat got closer.

"Base to sea horse 1, base to sea horse 1," the radio on the boat burst into life. "Sea Horse 1 to base, receiving over." Saunders's voice came down the line, "Can you see anything yet?" "No, not yet. Base, the target is stationary, no sign of life." "Approach with caution; your boarding party is ready." "Yes, base already." "Base to Sea Horse 1, be careful out." Saunders looked at the others, "Well, we wait."

On the patrol boat, tension was also rising; the sergeant piloting the boat was giving regular updates to the boarding party, the leader, another sergeant, slowly getting bored with the constant flow of information until he heard, "Get ready." He looked at the others, and they all released safety catches and moved to the side of the boat. Aboard the lucky lady, Alexander waited under his Tarpaulin.........

The police launch came alongside, and the boarders got ready. The pilot of the police launch nodded to the boarding party, and the next second, there was a cry, "Armed police" and the boarding party climbed on the "Lucky Lady." At that moment, Alexander threw off the tarpaulin and fired. He fired three shots; all three found targets. The sergeant fell back to the water, dead from a head shot; the second constable fell back in the launch with a chest wound. The third officer went in to cover his left shoulder, which was smashed. Alexander went looking for the fourth officer but never found them. Instead, he saw a glint in the corner of his eye, and he swung round to see Andy Silver standing by the cabin door, stunned, watching the scene. Alexander saw him but did not see that he had moved from his shadow cover to being lit by the light of the cabin; it was only seconds, only milliseconds, but it was enough. Two shots rang out; Robert Alexander, the Australian hitman for the Martinez Cartel, was dead, with two bullet wounds, both in the chest, both lethal.

On shore, there was pandemonium; they had heard the firefight, or rather the thirty-second gun battle that had taken place. But no radio contact; Saunders had tried to talk to the launch, but there was no response for what seemed like hours. It was only about two minutes. Then, the radio burst into life once again. ""Sea Horse 1 to base, 'Sea Horse 1 to base, the target is dead; we have one dead, two wounded, and one arrest made; request emergency help.'" "Base to Sea Horse 1 Base to Sea Horse 1, Wilco, ambulance there soon, come into marina area and dock will meet there, over." With that, the base party moved to the jetty. The time was four in the morning.

Southampton Port Office, Ocean Gate, Atlantic Way

"Is everything on schedule?" Singh looked at his watch. "Yes." Mary James also checked the time. She turned to Ben Williams, "Feeling ok?" Mary had noticed her deputy did not look well. "Doing ok, MA, am I?" Mary was doubtful,

though; Ben had been looking miserable since they had
arrived. She went through the plan in her head for about the
tenth time. The harbour master was to see the captain and
inform him of the drugs; Ben and his customs team would, at
the same time, go to the containers and start looking for the
drugs, which would not be too difficult as the containers had
been scratch-marked with a cross; Lomax, in his confession,
had drawn one on his confession.

At that moment, Singh, James, and Williams were joined
by Pete Barrington, the harbour master; he brought his
"mob," as he called them. Singh looked at the new arrivals; all
of them were big, burly men. Obviously, if there was trouble,
it would be sorted quickly. "Hi Pete, I see you brought the
boys along." Barrington smiled at the three people in front of
him, "Well, I have to prepare, you know." The man, who was
a tight head prop for his rugby club, now masquerading as a
customs officer, also looked at his watch. "It's five now; we
better go to the dockside. The group had been waiting inside
the building; now it was time to prepare the welcoming
committee, as Barrington put it.

The boat had come into the jetty, the dead had been
removed, the injured taken to hospital, and Andy Silver to a
police cell. Saunders surveyed the scene. It had been a result
not the one he wanted; he wanted the hitman alive, but it was
not to be, and probably given the resistance of the man, it
should not be surprising. He looked up; he saw Willis
approaching. "Well, you did it, boss." "Did what? I don't call
two dead and two wounded a resounding success." Willis
looked at his chief and wondered, in the few hours, if
Saunders had aged or seemed to have aged. The tall-looking
man seemed small; the blonde hair seemed a little grey, the

skin more wrinkled. Willis knew it could be so, but the effort of this, for some reason, all proved stressful for Saunders, he thought. Perhaps there is something else? Saunders looked at his watch; it said six, and the Southampton ship should be well on the way.

WESTERN DOCKS SOUTHAMPTON

Since Saunders had looked at his watch, the hour had passed quickly, or so it seemed to Jasleen Singh. Now, he was looking at the Sea Giant, and in truth, she was a giant, mainly because Singh had never been close to a ship like this, standing on a dockside. He looked to see the containers on deck and the crew, all two of them, so he could see on deck climbing over the containers. Then he heard a noise coming down the now lowered gangplank; it was a group of crewmen speaking English but in different accents. He was the group go. He saw Barrington and his team go up the plank and head for what he guessed was the ship's bridge. Next, he saw Ben Williams and two others go and head for the containers that left himself and Mary James. "Ladies first," and he moved aside as Mary started up the gangplank, the policeman bringing up the rear.

They got to the top of the gangplank and were soon joined by Barrington and the ship's captain, Ralf Meyer, from Hamburg, Germany. Barrington had had him arrested for the importation of drugs and was taking him for further questioning. "You do know, Captain, you are in serious trouble," Mary James looked at the grey-haired and bearded man who looked crushed at the news. "I know he replied in perfect accentless English. They watched the Germans go.

Then they heard Williams; he was walking quickly, and when they saw him, he had a triumphant look. "We got it, both containers, packed full. I don't know how much, but I have never seen anything like it." "Good; when can we deal with me?" Mary James slipped into operational mode. "Well, we have to unload and open the containers, then we will see how much". Then Williams paused. "Found this as well." He handed his boss a sheet of paper. Mary looked at it. "It's a receipt, but at the addresses from sender to receiver.".

Both Mary and Jasleen looked. The addresses were both in the same building. "So, what the same building does not mean is that any criminality has happened. Mary James looked annoyed at the apparent importance that Williams attached to his paper. Singh, however, clicked, "Where is the best place to hide a tree, in a wood, right?" Singh continued: "Two companies, same building, seemingly different but connected, the same man behind both, that is not important; what is important is you only need to go up or down in the lift; you can conduct business in safety within one building. No need for any communications that can be picked up by the good guys; it's all word of mouth.

CHAPTER TWENTY-ONE

National Crime Agency Units Citadel Place, London

It had been two days since the drugs were found, and Alexander was killed. It had been a time of sadness and joy. Sadness as the relatives of the dead and injured were informed, joy at finding the drugs and busting a gang. The three policemen sat around the table at a meeting called by Smith, who wanted to tie up any loose ends. "Well, I don't think there is anything more," Smith was about to close the meeting when Singh, who had been reading the final report, suddenly broke in, "Where did the information from the chess piece go?" "Does it matter?" Saunders chipped in while stirring a third tea. "What's the point?" added Smith.

"The point is," said Singh, "that we have a big loose end to tie up, and if we don't, we could be letting a big fish go." The other two looked on with curiosity; Smith then said, "Alright, what do we do?" "Find out where Alexander went and what he did. We interviewed the Silver brothers, and we know he, Alexander, took several trips; we just have to check traffic cameras." "One hell of a job," Smith observed. He went on, "What about the Mexicans?" "They are an American problem, not ours, and that is your department anyway." Singh's last point caught Smith off guard; he just grinned. "So check traffic cameras and find him." Saunders piped up, "Yes," Singh said. With that, the meeting broke up.

In fact, the "one hell of a job" turned out to be anything but; the car registration handed to the Thames Valley Police soon turned up, as the car Alexander had been driving had been caught on camera north of Oxford. A fine had been issued but had naturally arrived too late because the "Cornish Incident," as it had become known, had already taken place. Consequently, an appeal was launched after the meeting of the three detectives for the whereabouts of the car in connection with the Hampshire killings, and soon, a milkman said he spotted the car in the driveway of an investment banker who had farm milk delivered. The report fell onto Smith's desk first; he read it and asked to speak to Detective Chief Superintendent Alan Cartwright.

One hour later, Smith was in his boss's office. He handed the report to Cartwright, who skimmed through it quickly, and then Smith placed the all-important question in his mind: "What do we do about Sir Peter Derek?" He strengthened his case: "We know that Alexander went to see him probably to deliver the chess piece, and we know of Lomax's confession; both can be traced to Sir Peter." Cartwright listened and thought; to Smith, it seemed like long, slow minutes, but it was only a couple. Cartwright finally announced, "You and I will go and see him together; we ask him." "When" Smith seemed surprised at the senior officer's speed of action. "I will let you know." Cartwright looked his number two in the face, and Smith saw the look that said, "That's all." He left and awaited the decision. He did not have to wait long. One hour later he received a phone call; they were going tomorrow....

St Austell Police Station

Saunders was annoyed; he had been recalled to St Austell to log an evidence bag that had not been logged because of human error; it had been missed. Saunders was also annoyed that because of this, he had in his hands the one thing that could prove Sir Peter Derek and Alexander were together. He held in his hands a navigator found in Alexander's rucksack. He also had Smith's report. He also had a note from his sergeant that the navigator had a route to an Oxford address. He decided to ring London.

Smith was sitting at his desk when his phone rang; he looked at the number and saw it was Saunders.

"Hello Bob, what can I do for you?" "I have a navigator; Scots Detective finished the conversation. Smith, a few minutes later, was on the phone to Cartwright: We found it in Robert Alexander's rucksack. It has a route planned for a place in Oxford". "Really?" Smith suddenly paid attention. "Where?" he followed up. Saunders told him, and Smith guessed it was their destination in the morning, he thought, then said, "Ok Bob, leave it with me; I am going to see a witness at the address and let you know what happened." "Ok, good, good luck tomorrow."

Smith was deep in thought; they had been driving to the bankers with Cartwright driving. The thought that was in his head was the fact that Cartwright had not used his navigator or paid much attention to the road signs; could it be that Cartwright had been there before? Smith decided not to dwell on it, and he looked out of the window and watched as the M4 with straight lanes became the

A34 to Oxford, with the road twisting and turning through the villages, farmland, and woods of South Oxfordshire. They came to a "T" junction; on the other side of the road was a lane. Smith looked on as Cartwright looked left and right, then right and left, and drove straight across the road and down the lane. They drove for about five minutes. Soon, the lane opened up to a driveway, and at the end was a cottage with a thatched roof. Smith looked around; there was a front garden and a back garden, the wood here having been chopped down. Smith wondered who could have done it. He was still thinking when his thought was interrupted by Cartwright saying, "Come on, we are here."

The two men walked up to the cottage; Cartwright was about to press the bell when the door opened, and Smith and Cartwright were confronted by a tall, gaunt, older-looking man, about 60, as Smith thought, and looking unwell, as against himself and Cartwright, he a forty-year-old middle-distance runner when not a policeman, and Cartwright a Judoka, or Judo player, in his early fifties. Cartwright started the conversation: "Hello Peter, thank you for your time." "No problem, Alan, I have coffee or something stronger if you want," "Coffee will be just fine," Cartwright commented.

The three men went into the lounge; there was coffee and cups already out. Smith guessed that an agreement to talk had been reached, and it was to be here with coffee. "Well, Alan, what is this about?" "Well, Peter, we need to tie up a loose end. You had a visit from Robert Alexander recently; what was it about? Please tell us." "He was asking on behalf of a client about using my services to invest capital in a firm based in the USA.".

"Well, did you know that Alexander was a professional killer working for a Mexican drug cartel?" "No, I did not, and I have never dealt with a drug cartel." Smith listened, then played his card, catching both men off guard: "Well, Sir Peter, we found a navigator system with your address on it." "I have already told you." The banker was sounding angry; Smith landed the second blow. The cartel had an accountant, Mr. Lomax. Before he died, he wrote a confession about a chess piece and information about one of the Kings, the white one".

Cartwright had been watching this in disbelief; he found his voice: "Peter, if you know something, then tell us now." "I've told you what I know, now please go." The banker was looking cross, and Cartwright recognised he was rattled. He decided to stop the meeting. "Well, sorry to bother you, Peter, accept our apologies." The detectives drank their coffee and left.

Outside, Cartwright exploded in a raging torrent of anger. "Why didn't you tell me about the navigator and the confession?" "The confession was in the report on Alexander, but the navigator was new information." Cartwright was slightly mollified; Smith was right about the confession. Smith then asked, "Do you think he is guilty?" "Yes, I do," "How do we catch him? "Smith awaited an answer. "Well, first, we talk to the Silver Brothers again; this time, we talk about drugs and not just our dead killer." "But we did talk about drugs," "Yes, but not so much," countered Cartwright, "we do it again.

CHAPTER TWENTY-TWO

Hampshire Police Headquarters

The interview room was like interview rooms all over Britain, four chairs a table and a tape recorder. The four men had been there for five minutes the first two arriving on their own. The second two were brought by uniformed officers. Now Singh and Smith, for the law-and-order community, stood against the Silver Brothers. "I want you to tell us about the drugs and the plan to import". Daniel Smith opened the interview the way he wanted, straight to the point. "We told you what we know" Andy Silver glared at the detectives. Singh continued the line, "But we want to know specifically about the drugs, that's all".

Tommy Silver parried the thrust, "What's in it for us?". "We want a deal before we say anything". Smith had seen this coming, and he reposted. "We can do that, but before we do, we want answers to two questions". Andy answered, "Alright, but where is our lawyer". "He'd be here soon". Singh slipped the words in, taking his cue from his partner and ending his sentence. The brothers looked at each other, and then Andy placed the question the detectives wanted. "What do you want to know." "First, we found this address on a navigator. Do you know it, and did you give it to Alexander?" "Yes", said Andy I do know it. I googled it". Smith listened and made notes, and he then asked his second question, "Tell me about this chess set thing".

Tommy answered quickly. "Well, I met with two other men in a Premier Inn Hotel near Terminal 3 London

Heathrow, ""Did you know them," Smith asked. "Yes, I knew them; the man with the set was called Cardenas, and the other was a bodyguard. I was the British end of the network." "Ok, continue" Smith smelt blood. "I was told to give the chess set to the man I know as David Lomax". I got one of my youngsters to hand Lomax the set, but as we know, he lost it". Smith looked at the brothers; he looked at the file in front of him, he then signalled to the uniforms who had been in the room to take the Silver twins away. The twins protested about the deal they wanted; Smith only promised to look into the possibility.

When the twins had gone, Smith turned to Singh. "Alright, you make the arrest of Sir Peter Derek; Cartwright can't because of personal knowledge, and I can't because I am tied to Cartwright because of his knowledge of the suspect. It was originally your case". "No problem, we will pick him up tonight".

Singhs team picked Sir Peter Derek up at the cottage. Faced with Tommy Silvers's statement and the navigator, he slowly but surely confessed. Singh later said it was the prospect of losing respectability that caused him to confess; he added that it was too late for the accused to worry about social standing.

Later in the early evening Singh and Smith talked about the case and were pleased they had wound up the network in the UK. Smith joked they could go after the Mexicans; Singh told him they were probably fighting between themselves over the loss of the drugs; he and Smith had nothing to worry about.

The Hilton Hotel "Reforma" Mexico City.

The sun was rising on Mexico City, another hot spring day, and for the people of the city, smog-filled pollution began to take hold. But for the two men in the hotel room, this did not matter, they had a decision to make and make it quickly, for their enemies were closing in. "Well, there it is. That is our only option left if the cartel is to survive, drink Amigo". Miguel, the shadow, poured out two whiskies, Antonio. Cardenas took his glass and, sitting on the bed pondered what the cartels legal adviser had said. Miguels argument was simple, the plan had fallen apart, and Martinez had become a hermit again not being seen for days, and with Alexander the "Verdugo" or executioner in English dead and no longer the terror he was the other cartels started whittling away The Acapulco empire. Now the situation was dangerous for the two men in the hotel room.

Cardenas sipped his drink, "Ok so what do we do"? "You take control of the Cartel; Martinez has to die". Cardenas looked at the man called the shadow and realized he was staying in the shadow, not doing anything to expose himself. Yes, he was well named Cardenas thought, his next thought came aloud. "Who is going to kill him". "I have that organised", Miguel sipped his drink he then had an afterthought: "The English knight, he is talking freely, it could be dangerous". "You mean Sir Peter Derek" Cardenas thought aloud "yes" Miguel finished his whiskey. Cardenas then asked, "what do we do with him". "Kill him also we must tie up the loose ends". "How we do that, kill I mean",

Cardenas finished his drink. Miguel smiled, "all under control Amigo", go home and wait a day.

The Casa Dorada Acapulco

Martinez was lying on the bed in his cottage meant for guests, his mind was spinning over and over. It had been ten days since the world, according to Martinez, had started to fall apart; it had started with Alexander's death and then the capture of the drugs, and finally the arrest of Derek; all this had brought the Cartel and Martinez to the edge of destruction, and of all the misfortune it was the death of Alexander the "Verdugo" who literally did wipe out the opposition that had caused the most problems with Alexander went opponents now had a chance, and they took it.

True, Cardenas was number two, but it was Alexander who made sure it was Martinez reigned; now it was all over. Martinez got off the bed and opened the window to the bedroom; he had been hiding there for ten days, hoping to think of a way out as the empire he had created fell apart; he still had his "soldiers" but they were not Alexander, for his named spread terror, he did not even have to be in a place, his name was enough, now it was gone. He thought further, the speed of the collapse was due to the English Knight, he had been arrested was talking freely betraying everything, and because he had helped Martinez move in political and aristocratic society and spread the tentacles of the cartel, those societies that had accepted his drugs had now found him a problem and to survive they were fighting back against the invader, their weapons were law enforcement and other Cartels using their own connections to split up his empire.

He went to the bathroom, showered, and look in the mirror, he seemed older, is hair greyer, and the skin more wrinkled, he had aged, he felt shorter more hunched up. He was contemplating when he heard the front door alarm. He went to the door and watched screen attached to the camera that covered the front door.

He saw the slim figure, jet-black crew cut hair of Rafael the police chief. "Hi, Rafael, why the personal call, Martinez was wondering why the policeman was here without being requested to visit. The policeman answered, "I have news of the English Knight, we must talk". Martinez thought more, Cardenas had been sent to Mexico City to see Miguel, and had not come back yet, Miguel his "fixer" had not said a word. He looked at the screen, "Ok wait a minute" as he told the officer, he pressed a button, the door opens automatically, he went to greet the visitor, "Come", he did not finish the sentence, he was transfixed by the pistol with the silencer, two shots were fired, as Martinez fell he saw the sun glassed face of the police man looking at him. The policeman then turned away, First Inspector Rafael Jimenez, dialled a number, it rang, a voice appeared "yes", "It is done", "alright" the voice responded. The policeman finished the call and left.

Sir Peter Dereks Cottage

The English knight as the Mexicans called him, was in his office working on an investment deal, he had been very lucky to be granted bail, the judge had accepted he would surrender his passport and report to the police twice a week. He had been interviewed and he had cooperated fully, he had even been asked about Benjamin Williams, for he had been caught when Tommy Silvers phone had been found with his message on it. However, Peter Derek knew nothing.

Furthermore, with his clever lawyer and a prosecution lawyer whose boss knew the Knight as a golf partner and fellow cocaine user, he figured he would stay at liberty for a long time.

He continued his work; he had put the radio on and listened to a local morning radio show and worked on the spreadsheet; he worked away until the ten O'clock news came on. He was only half listening when he suddenly stopped; a news story had come about a suspected Cartel leader killed. His name was Juan Martinez. Derek began to feel sick; with Martinez dead, was he next? He wondered what to do, ring the police, run for himself, he thought about it and decided to run.

He went upstairs to pack a bag but did not get the chance; his doorbell rang. He went to the living room window and looked out; he recognised two detectives who had been part of the investigation team, Detective Sergeants Sarah Campbell and David Whittam. He waved, and they waved back; he went to the door, opened it and let the two detectives in. "I am glad you're here. Have you heard the news"? "Yes, we have; that's why we are here; we are going to take you to a safe house; we have clothes and things already, just need you; we can bring other things later if needed.

Sir Peter relaxed as Whittam led the way to their car; they got in, Whittam in the driving seat, Sir Peter front passenger seat, and Campbell behind. They started off. After fifteen minutes, Whittam said, "I need to pee; there is a picnic spot with a toilet nearby. "They were soon there; Whittam got out, and so did the other two. Whittam disappeared, and Campbell and Derek were left alone. "You be safe soon", Campbell smiled again as Derek relaxed, no danger, he thought. He looked happily at the detective. He noticed she was looking in her handbag, and he looked up as he heard Whittam come back; he was about to make small talk when he heard Campbell, "Sir Peter" Derek looked up but only heard two shots. He fell to the ground. Campbell looked at the body, made a phone report in and then she and Whittam left. Acapulco had a very long reach. The murders of Derek and Martinez remain unsolved.